The Adventures of
Charlie Conti

SMALL SACRIFICES

BEN LANGDON
ELIZA LANGDON

ILLUSTRATED BY LORIN OLSEN

KALAMITYPRESS

Published by Kalamity Press, Portland Australia
kalamitypress.com

Copyright © 2016 Ben Langdon

ISBN: 978-0-9875308-8-2

Cover design and all illustrations by Lorin Olsen.

Interior design by Polgarus Studio.

Dedications

This is dedicated to the grandmothers, each of whom have helped shape the writers, and the people, we've become. To Diane, who kindled the love of reading in her grandchildren by narrating dozens of audio cassettes which we devoured in the semi-darkness of nap time. To Bertha, who always wanted the very best for us. To Megan, who did it on her own and showed the power of education and the beauty of gardens and winding brick paths. And to Kate, who also did it on her own, and opened up the amazing world of cooking and telling it how it is.

Thank you, from Ben and Eliza.

Illustrator's Dedication

Illustrations dedicated to Ben and Eliza Langdon. Thank you so much for this opportunity, for letting me be a part of bringing Charlie Conti and all her friends to life, and most of all for your kindness and friendship. I cannot tell you what a pleasure it has been to work with you. I knew from the very first portrait I did for you that this was something special.

Lorin Olsen

My Family... 😐

THIS ISN'T A story about a normal girl.

Don't get me wrong, I would love to be a normal girl, but considering my dad is a professional, unionised minion and has worked for such villainous luminaries as the Crash and Burn Twins, Doctor Death (the Third and Fourth versions), Yellow Peril and Captain Calamari, chances of living out my life with any kind of normality are pretty slim. I'm surprised our family has survived this long.

My name's Charlie Conti and I'm fourteen years old. I'm a bit of a nerd, I guess, because my role models are Marie Curie and Maryam Mirzakhani instead of Miley Cyrus or any of the Kardashians. I guess I have a bit of a mad scientist streak in me, although I have no interest in taking over the world or anything.

I just want to live the regular kind of life.

And that brings me to this story.

You see, my dad has dragged me and my little brother, Luca, away from Melbourne where I've spent most of my life so far. Out of the Light and into the Darkness of regional Victoria to a coastal town called Henty Bay.

Yeah, I'd never heard of it either.

I can see the benefits though. After all the problems with the Port Melbourne Intifada, where Captain Calamari totally lost it and my dad ended up at the bottom of Port Phillip Bay, we had to leave the city. There were some harsh words thrown around and maybe a few vendettas were forged in the fires of the moment.

So we had to move. Dad, or The Undertaker as he's known in the business, was damaged goods. The most he could hope for if he stayed in Melbourne would have been prolonged unemployment. The more likely outcome would have been a long stay in prison or a knife in the back.

I'm not being melodramatic. These kinds of things do happen.

The family's new plan is to move to Henty Bay so Luca and I can grow up and live normal lives. Maybe even go to university and get an office job with superannuation and a chance to grow old without having to worry about dodging laser beams and undead Vikings. My brother and I have our own little dreams. Luca wants a puppy, or a bearded dragon lizard thing; and I just want to stay longer than six months in the one school.

I told you I was a nerd.

Chapter One
Living above Momma Cho's

MOMMA CHO'S CHINESE Restaurant took up two shop fronts on the main street. The signage was a bit faded but there was a spectacular mural running along the bottom of the windows depicting a twisting green dragon. Flecks of gold scales sparkled in the light as we stood there out front. My dad checked his phone again to make sure the address was right.

"It's a Chinese restaurant," I said as Luca pressed his face to the window.

"No, no," Dad said, swiping his finger across the screen. "Ah, yes."

He looked at the front door again, then put a hand on my shoulder, giving it a bit of a squeeze.

"No, no, yes?" I asked. "Really?"

"It's going to be stellar," Dad said.

The door to the restaurant opened with the jingle of bells and a woman came out, eyes squinting in the sun. She had nice round cheeks and after giving us all the up and down glance, she smiled widely.

"Mister Contee," she said, stretching the 'ee' sound. "You late."

Dad shrugged and picked up one of the suitcases. He reached out and shook Momma Cho's hand. She laughed, let it go quickly, and then scooped up Luca bringing him right up to her face like she was going to sniff him.

Luca froze, his whole body going limp.

And then Momma Cho gave him a big hug and placed him back on the ground. She was a strong woman.

"You lucky to have boy," she said to Dad, giving me only a sideways glance. "I have four girls. Nothing but trouble."

I figured I should have been insulted, but seriously, after the smells of the restaurant followed Momma Cho out into the street I really didn't mind if she called me a serial killer. I probably would have gladly killed someone for food right then. Instead, I shoved my hands into my pockets and looked up above the shopfront to where our apartment was hidden away.

"You go through that door," Momma Cho said, handing Dad the key which was swathed in red ribbon, presumably so he wouldn't lose it. "And I send Jade up to bring you food."

"Thank you," Dad said softly. And then the fire cracker that was Momma Cho withdrew back to the restaurant, leaving the three of us on the footpath.

"Let's get going," I said. "The suspense is killing me."

"Literally," Luca added and I grinned at him.

It was a running joke between us. He had no idea what it meant but it made me laugh every time. Dad had no trouble with our luggage. He used to do this party trick where he juggled bowling balls. One of the side benefits of being The Undertaker was that Dad had been a test subject for more than one mad scientist. Whatever they'd done to his body, they'd maxed out his muscles so he could easily lift a small car above his head. And, yes, that's another one of his party tricks. Dad unlocked the front door, which was an inconspicuous black colour, and the three of us peered up into a dark stairwell.

"Looks mysterious," Dad said, drawing out the word with a mischievous grin. "Who's going up first?"

"Me!" shouted Luca, bolting past Dad, and dragging his Cartoon Network suitcase behind him. Even after the six hour drive the little kid was full of energy. Dad looked at me and must have seen my lack of enthusiasm. He roughed up my hair a bit and then picked up everything we owned.

"He's just like his Uncle Jesse," Dad said. "Always rushing into the unknown."

The last time I'd seen Uncle Jesse, he was waving to me from behind the plexi-glass window of a shuttle about to be launched into another dimension. It didn't make me feel any better.

"Let's go, kiddo," he said.

We trudged up the flight of stairs in almost darkness. The walls were painted dark and it felt like we were climbing up a steep tunnel. It smelled a bit wet too, like being underground.

When I got to the landing, Dad and Luca had already burst into the apartment. I couldn't find the same excitement, and as I stood in the doorway the first thing I noticed was the strange smell, like wet dog. It wasn't a surprise. I stepped inside and dropped the bags, my eyes moving slowly around the apartment. The walls of the combined kitchen-lounge-dining area were lime green. There was a battered faux-leather sofa, an old-style chunky television, a round dining table from the 1950s with four mostly matching chairs and a beanbag which looked only half-stuffed. The kitchen was a bench and a couple of old appliances. There was a sink and a half-sized refrigerator. On the bench was a microwave. There wasn't an oven. Nonna would have crossed herself and fainted at that. No house is a home without an oven, she used to say. I realised I was still hungry and nearly turned around to go back down the stairs, out of this place.

But then I saw the window. It was big, covering the width of the living area and outside the sun was bright and warm. The sky was that perfect kind of blue, and best of all, I could see the ocean. I left our cases by the door and walked to the window. Luca was laughing in the bedroom shouting something about finding a PlayStation, and Dad was investigating the bathroom. It was kind of peaceful with their noises subdued by walls, and looking out over the roofs of the other buildings, I could see the blue-green of the ocean.

A real ocean.

I pressed my hands against the glass and noticed it move a little. My heart nearly exploded and I pulled back, fully expecting to collapse through the glass and to my death, but it only wobbled. I pressed again, slowly, and felt a little embarrassed. The window was a sliding door.

"You're not supposed to go out there," a voice called behind me. "It's not finished."

I turned around and saw a girl standing in the doorway carrying two bulging white plastic bags of take-away food. She was about my age and wore a button-up white shirt and a black skirt.

"Um, okay," I said, stepping back from the window.

"I'm Jade, from downstairs," the girl said. "Pleased to meet you. Mum wanted me to bring this up for you guys. She's really big on feeding the world, you know?"

"I'm Charlie," I said. The smells reached me and I felt the hunger rise again. Luca jumped out of the door to the bedroom and growled, fingers bent like raptor talons.

Jade raised her eyebrows and smiled.

"You must be 'the boy'," she said.

"Oh he's the boy alright," I said. "Good to meet you, and thanks for the food. I think I could eat the whole thing right now. Thanks."

"No problem," Jade said.

"Are there fortune cookies?" Luca asked, taking a bag and sliding himself onto a chair at the table.

"Sorry. Sichuan prawns, combination hokkein noodles and mixed vegetables, spring rolls and I think Sang Cho Bau."

"Sick," Luca said. "And rice."

"Thanks," I said, knowing I'd already said it.

"And Sprite," Jade added as Luca twisted the lid from the bottle and the soft drink sprayed his face, bursting through the lid. "Sorry about that, I kind of ran up the stairs."

Luca licked his face and started clawing into the rice.

"That's cool," I said. "How much do we owe you?"

Jade waved her hand and stepped back to the door.

"It's on the house," she said with a smile. "Mum always says 'it's on the house', because she thinks it's funny."

She paused, waiting for something. I felt a little awkward and the smells were pulling me towards the table.

"Because you're above the shop?" Jade offered. "On the house?"

"Oh, right," I said. "That's pretty funny."

"For my mum, that's a laugh-riot. You'll get used to it. I'll leave you guys. I've got to get back to work, but if you need anything just come down to the restaurant."

And then she was gone. I could hear the clip-clap of her shoes as she ran downstairs again.

I slipped into the seat next to Luca and pulled out a plastic tub of noodles and prawns. We looked at each other for a second, both of us smiling. Luca's face was smeared with a dark plum sauce, reaching from the corner of his mouth towards his left eye. He looked ridiculous, as usual.

"Welcome to our new home, little brother," I said.

There was the sound of a flushing toilet.

I took a mouthful of the noodles and laughed as Dad came stumbling into the main room. He was wearing his comic-style boxers, black t-shirt and bare feet.

"Make yourself at home, Dad?"

"This is going to be great," he said, stretching. "Did you two make dinner?"

Luca nodded.

"This is the best family ever," he declared, and then sat down on a chair which squeaked under his weight. He stood up again and gave it a cursory glance, lifting it up and frowning.

He moved to the other chair, next to me.

"I think we'll save that chair for visitors," he said, and then reached for the food. "Let's eat, Conti family."

Chapter Two
Rooftop Conversation

IT'S NIGHT. YOU can tell because the whole main street of this town is empty and you can actually see the stars in the sky. The only sound I can hear is the distant thunder of the beach. I can imagine the waves tumbling up the sand, never stopping, never slowing.

I think you'd like it here, Mum.

I'm sitting on the roof above the Chinese restaurant. It's not really a balcony - just a corrugated iron roof that dips a little when you sit on it. The sliding door from our apartment just opens up onto it, kind of like it's hoping to one day magically reveal a sophisticated townhouse balcony instead of rusted tin and open sky. Luca's not allowed out here and Dad thinks he'd probably fall through it if he tried, so it's my own little place.

And it's nice out here.

Dad's gone out to make a phone call. He says he can't trust his mobile and the apartment doesn't have a landline. I suggested he use mine, but you know Dad, he doesn't want to use anything that you gave me. Besides, I think the battery is dead.

I know that yesterday I hated the whole idea of this

place, this little seaside town halfway between Melbourne and Adelaide, right slap-bang in the middle of nowhere. But I guess it's not so bad. Luca and I went for a walk after we ate dinner. There's a few nice shops you'd probably like. There's even this really old fashioned lolly shop where they sell ginger fudge like Grandma used to love. Luca rubbed his face against the window of a comic shop, so that's another good sign, and there's a little library behind the civic hall which I'll have to visit when I don't have Luca pulling me every other way.

School's a different story. We didn't see it today, but apparently it's across a lagoon which is populated with tiger snakes and maybe even a crocodile. The girl from downstairs told us that, but she laughed when she did and I don't know her well enough to tell if she's joking. Turns out she's in the same year as me and she's promised to help me fit in.

Yeah, she seems nice. Maybe a bit naive, but maybe I'm too cynical.

Luca's school is right next door to the high school so that'll help with drop-offs and pick-ups. Dad says he'll have it all under control, but … yeah … we all know how this will turn out. I bought a new lunch box for Luca when we were down the street too. It's got a dinosaur on the front, which won't be any kind of surprise to you, I guess.

So, yeah, I think this place isn't as bad as I thought.

It's not Melbourne.

I don't know anyone here except Jade, but I guess since we move all the time this won't be any better or worse than the other places. It would be nice to stay in one spot for more than six months though.

I know, I'm exaggerating.

I'm fourteen so I think it's pretty much okay to exaggerate, especially when tomorrow is the first day of a new high school. I won't have a uniform (no surprise), but Dad has filled out the enrolment forms so it should be a smooth enough transition. I'll probably have to fast talk the administration a little bit, but you know it won't be the first time. People don't like to look too closely at potential problems.

I wish you were closer.

I remember when you walked me to prep on the first day of school. You wouldn't let go of my hand and I had to dig in my nails to make you drop. I was a little demon, I know. It's funny how I remember that day so clearly - the dash through the gates, the near-head-on collision with that

Stephens kid, and then the classroom. All the smells and the colours are still right here in my mind.

And you too.

You were there, always just watching me, worrying about me. Listening to my wild stories and carrying my bag.

I just wish you were here now. I remember your perfume when I close my eyes and it always makes me feel empty. Like now, even in this beautiful night, there's a really big piece of life that's not here.

And it's you, Mum.

It's always you.

Chapter Three
Morning Drop-Off

"I HAVE TO go now or I'll be late," I said.

Dad didn't move. He had the Reducer resting in his hands at the table and he'd been sitting like that without moving for nearly an hour. He hadn't shaved. He was still wearing his ridiculous superhero boxer shorts and Luca was still in the shower singing pop songs with his head full of shampoo and hair conditioner.

"Dad, I don't need this right now," I said, grabbing for the Reducer which was really just an over-sized ray gun. He'd picked it up cheap before the mess with Captain Calamari. I pulled it away from him but he still looked like he was asleep with his eyes open. "Can you please just get up and help me?"

I slid the Reducer to the other end of the table and snatched the loaf of bread for sandwiches. As I sliced and spread and selected like a professional, I kept looking back to Dad and cursing him under my breath. So it wasn't a surprise when I cut my finger on the sandwich wrap dispenser. I shook it hard to keep from swearing louder and reached for the tin of band-aids while sucking on the cut, trying not to let it bleed out too much. Dad didn't move. I managed to cover the cut and finish the sandwiches, squishing mine a bit too much as I shoved it into my lunch box alongside a fruit juice box and two Mars bars. Without chocolate I was never going to survive the day.

Luca walked into the room bare naked, still singing a Taylor Swift song. He gave me a very relaxed thumbs up and disappeared into the bedroom.

I looked at Dad but he was still staring at the table as if trying to decode an ancient alien text. He'd done something to the Reducer. There were a few components loose; sitting on the table like little plastic beads. Dad wasn't an inventor. He was more of a tinkerer, and nine times out of ten he was simply a destroyer; things he played with never worked the same again.

"It's nearly nine o'clock," I said, but it was no use. No one was listening to me. I dropped Luca's lunch into his bag and shoved in a jumper, just in case it got cold. Then, since the bathroom was empty, I ducked in and looked at myself in the misted-up mirror. I wiped my forearm across the surface, revealing a normal looking girl.

I seriously looked normal.

I had normal brown hair, done up in a normal pony tail. My eyes were also a very normal brown and I had normal looking skin - no sign of adolescent pimples and somewhere just a shade away from the olive complexion of my father's side of the family.

I blinked, but when my eyes opened again I was just as normal.

My clothes would look out of the ordinary though. We

hadn't had time to shop for proper school uniform, but I'd decided on a plain white shirt and jeans.

"Are you ready yet?" Luca asked from the doorway. "We're going to be late."

His head was still wet and his hair stuck up at the back. He hadn't brushed his teeth or even had any breakfast but he was raring to go. I grabbed him and pulled him to the basin. In a swift and practised motion I squirted some toothpaste on his brush and he started scrubbing away, still with that pop song somehow coming through it all. I brushed my own teeth and tried to fix his hair at the same time.

In all the chaos we managed to get everything done. Except breakfast, but that wasn't anything out of the ordinary. There wasn't an oven in the apartment anyway, or a toaster.

We grabbed our bags and left the apartment. Luca yelled out a goodbye to Dad but I didn't even bother. He'd come home late the night before while I was still out on the rooftop. There'd been some kind of important phone call, and that was code for a 'work issue'. He had slumped onto the sofa and started drinking beer, so I had stayed out in the night air listening to the waves at the beach I hadn't even seen yet.

And it was at that time, somewhere around 1am, that I saw the boy on the bike. The streets were empty for the whole time I was up there, but then - from out of nowhere - this kid came speeding down the middle of the road on a BMX. He zoomed across right below where I was sitting, then did this amazing hard left turn, skidding like a

professional stunt rider, and taking off again down the street that led to the beach.

It happened in less than a minute but it still played re-runs in my head.

Luca and I got out onto the main street and I felt better, even though we were definitely going to be late. I knew the way to the schools, thanks to Google Maps, but there was no way we would make the trip and sign in within the five minutes we had before the bells would ring for the start of school. Instead of freaking out, I took a piece of advice my Nonna was so fond of dishing out at Christmas. All things will come to pass. Rushing them only makes a mess. And it was true. If I rushed to get Luca to school, I'd make a mistake.

And we couldn't afford mistakes. Not anymore.

We stopped at the bakery and got two croissants for breakfast. Luca wanted a sticky bun but I figured a croissant was less hopeless as breakfast than a bun sprinkled with hundreds and thousands. We ate silently as we walked, and the town sort of slipped away as we approached the lagoon.

It was like a park with a lake in it, except the lake was actually a tidal lagoon, complete with fish, birds, reeds, tiger snakes and a crocodile, if we were to believe Jade Cho. And I didn't. At least not about the crocodile.

"Dad was grumpy today," Luca said, as we walked across a wooden bridge with wild reeds growing on either side. A pelican cruised on the water just ahead of us, its ridiculous beak trembling like it had just swallowed a fish, or a small cat.

"He had a late night," I said.

"Do you think he'll pick me up from school?"

I shrugged and finished my pastry. Luca didn't really need an answer. He was eight years old and he'd known Dad his whole life. Instead of worrying about it, Luca picked off one of the reeds and started swishing it from side to side like a sword, running a little ahead of me with his bulging backpack bouncing up and down. I smiled. He was having a good time. The sun was shining.

It wasn't the end of the world.

We got to the primary school ten minutes after the first class had started but the woman at the office didn't seem upset or angry or even the least bit surprised. She smiled at us and fussed about with the enrolment forms.

"You'll be with Mrs Ursa and the 2s, just down there," she said with an officious point of her finger. She shuffled the forms I'd given her into a folder and then slipped them out of view. "That's all we need for today. You'd better get to class, Luca. I can take him if you like."

"Nah, that's cool," I said. "I'd like to do it."

She smiled again and handed me an envelope.

"It's our little 'Welcome to Power Street Primary School' kit. There's information on uniform, where to buy it and … well, we're a Sun Smart school, so there are rules about hats and…"

She waved her hand and laughed.

"Lots of reading for your mum and dad," she added.

I smiled back at her and then we headed towards Luca's room. There was already the familiar buzz of a primary school - distant chanting of welcome songs, sudden bursts of sounds and the occasional little person running off to the toilet. When we got to Mrs Ursa's room, Luca had already shaken off his bag and was ready to bolt right into things. He didn't seem to care that he knew no one, that he'd left his old school and old friends behind. It was like he'd shed a skin, and this was a whole new, outgoing and fun Luca Conti.

I watched from the doorway as Mrs Ursa accepted Luca onto the carpet at the front of the room. She made eye contact with me and winked. She was like a very large brown bear - her cardigan was enormous and her bobbed hair was streaked with reds and browns. She had a huge, honey voice too. Luca looked over his shoulder at me, which I thought was a nice gesture, even though he was probably more worried about my first day than his own. I gave him a wave and then hung up his bag on a hook by the door. The kids on the floor started singing a welcome song and added new names every time it went around the circle.

I slipped back into the corridor.

It was my turn now.

Chapter Four
Would Charlene Conti,
Please Stand Up?

IT TOOK ME less than an hour to fill in the rest of my forms, convince the administration people that my dad wasn't a reprobate blow-in from the 'big city' and settle into Maths class with a man who looked suspiciously like a walrus. Yes, that was a long-winded description of my entry into Henty Bay Secondary College. Now you know how I felt - it was seriously like a whirlwind.

I had missed the orientation into high school, so all the kids seemed to know each other and all about how the school worked. It's amazing how turning up two hours late to your first day of school can really screw things up.

Thanks Dad.

The class itself was pretty small. There were sixteen kids: mostly a mix of blonde heads. It was like the entire town was straight out of a surf film. Except for Jade Cho, who had jet black hair, and this other kid who had a strange purple-black hair thing going on. Funnily enough, that kid sat by himself at the back of the room. I got to sit at the front.

Because I was late.

Thanks Dad. Again.

"Bailey?" the Walrus asked. "Fin Bailey?"

"Yeah," a kid said, raising her hand straight up.

"Cho?"

I shot a look at Jade who was off to my right near the window, and she gave me the thumbs-up. She was chewing gum, but when the teacher called her full name she masterfully replied without giving it away.

"Right here, sir," she said.

The Walrus nodded and made another note in his journal. While he was going about his book keeping, most of the kids seemed to be having conversations which had started before my arrival. Considering most of them had grown up together, the same conversations had probably been going on for months, or years. I felt a little out of my depth.

"Conti?" the Walrus asked again and I sunk lower into my chair. I hadn't realised just how embarrassing the first day at a new school could be, which is strange because I'd had a lot of 'first days' in my life.

"Charlene Conti?"

I started to raise my hand but it was a half-hearted attempt.

"Yes," I said, but he didn't hear. Probably because a couple of the girls right behind me started laughing. I dropped my hand completely, hiding it in my lap under the desk.

"Would Charlene Conti please stand up?" he asked, looking at the class over his eye glasses.

There was no way I was going to stand up.

Zero chance.

I folded my arms across my chest and stayed as low as I could. The girls behind me stopped chattering, but one of them kicked the back of my chair. The Walrus looked across the room and then sighed a little, bending down to write something in his journal.

Charlene had been my mum's idea. I can't really forgive her for that, even after everything that happened later. There should be classes for new parents, about the naming of their children. What seems like a good idea at the time, probably really isn't in the real world. Charlene was this spunky character on some television soap opera years ago. Mum and Dad spent a lot of their time together in front of the television in Dad's caravan when they first got together. He lived out the back of his parents' house and their love kind of blossomed alongside the melodrama they watched on the TV.

The major casualty of their soap-inspired life was me.

Charlene Bianca Louise Conti.

But everyone calls me Charlie.

At least that is generally the plan.

After being marked absent in Maths I headed out to lunch with the rest of the school, but it's pretty hard to find a group when everyone's already formed up. Kids shifted as we moved outside. Some went to the canteen and sat around enjoying the sun and each other's company. Others kicked around a football. The older kids already had their spaces, and they sat in their spots like some kind of choreographed painting.

I found myself sitting against the concrete wall of the bike shed.

At least I had my Mars bar.

It didn't take too long for the silence to be broken. I'd only just pulled back a part of the wrapper when I heard a crash. Metal and something. It was quickly followed by some shouts just around the corner of the shed. I probably should have just sat there, but I was tired of waiting for the end of the day to roll on by, so I pulled myself up and stepped to the edge of the bike shed. The concrete walls were warm and I pressed my fingers around the corner to get a good look.

Three beach-blonde boys were messing around on scooters. Two of them were wearing the school uniform, but the third one was wearing a flannelette shirt, unbuttoned and flapping behind him as he lifted his scooter into the air and twisted it into some skater-move.

I had no idea what it was called, but I'd been living close to skate parks in the city, so I knew they liked to get altitude and didn't much care about how they landed.

I stepped down to the concrete floor and leaned against the wall. The boys noticed me but they didn't say anything, and they didn't seem put-off by my appearance. They just kind of ignored me. I took a bite of the chocolate and watched them, semi-consciously calculating their movements, predicting their falls. It's amazing what you can do with Maths when you're effectively an invisible spectator.

One of the school boys flipped his scooter up as he landed awkwardly, the wheels shooting into the air again, although he held on to the bars. He stumbled a few steps and then swept the scooter back under his control, stopping right next to me.

A burst of energy washed over me - his face was shiny with sweat, his eyes wide and alive. I could feel his hot breath. It was a boy.

"Wow," he said, flashing his bright white teeth in a smile. "That was intense."

I nodded.

"Can I have a bite of your Mars bar?"

Before I could answer, the boy reached out and touched my hand, bringing the chocolate towards him. He ducked his head quickly and took a bite, pulling back with wide, appreciative eyes.

"Thanks," he said, and swept back into the shed, careening around in a wide arc, bending low and then lifting off the ground in a little leap.

I think I nearly died.

Instead, I sort of slipped back around the edge of the shed and went back to sit on the grass.

I looked around the yard and didn't see anything different. A couple of kids were wrestling on the grass over a football, and a bunch of girls were sunning their legs and passing around their phones.

My Mars bar was bitten.

I didn't know how I felt about that.

But then the bell went, and we all drifted back into the school. Jade caught up with me at the lockers and waited for me while I rummaged through my bag for a new binder book.

"We've got History," Jade said. "Should be a breeze and then we can get out of here. Can you believe that we've only been here for, like, less than one day?"

I shrugged and closed my locker.

"I don't know," I said. "Hard to keep track of things, what with all the excitement."

She mock-punched my arm and laughed.

"You should come and check out the restaurant sometime. I can get you a job there if you want, but you know, you'd be better off not. My mum is … well, she works everyone really hard."

I smiled. Jade was talking to me like we'd known each other for years. We walked down the hall and she told me all about her family - her sisters, her dad, even her aunt who was in a wheelchair because she'd fallen out of a helicopter.

"Been there," I muttered, and then we were in class. Jade sat at the front and pulled me next to her as I walked in. I dropped to the seat with a bigger smile on my face. It was a strange feeling being wanted.

"Hey," a boy said, as he walked in and headed to the next row. It was the scooter boy from lunch, although he'd tucked in his white shirt and was wearing the school jumper. I turned around to watch him. He smiled.

"That's Will," Jade said. "I dated him in Grade Four, long story."

"Oookay," I said, watching Will line up his pens: red, blue, blue, black, red. The boy had a lot of pens. His hair was long at the front and kept falling into his eyes as he straightened the pens. It was sun-touched, like his warm face with a sprinkling of freckles…

"Welcome to History," a teacher called from the door, and I nearly slammed my knees into the top of the table. "Let's hope we don't repeat her mistakes, but learn and adapt from those who have gone before."

I turned around. The teacher was a woman wearing a blue and yellow summer dress. Her skin was tanned and she didn't mind showing it off. It was like the entire town had enjoyed a summer of sunshine and light. They were all so bright and happy and alive.

My family had spent the summer hiding in a basement, and then a few weeks in a shipping container. I could see the difference it had made.

"We're lucky to have a exhibition in town," the teacher said as she swept herself up to sit on the front desk, swinging her bronze legs to the side like some kind of mythical queen. If we were going to study the Ancient Egyptians and Cleopatra I think I would have laughed out loud. She looked the part already. "Our sister city in Mexico has brought out a new, albeit quite small, collection of Aztec artifacts. You wouldn't have been here three years ago when we received the last visit, but, oh my Goddess, it was divine."

She shook her shoulder-length black hair and then focused on the class.

"I'm Miss Monzote, but you can call me Mara," she said. "As long as the principal isn't within ear shot." She laughed and then pulled out her purse. With a click of the latch she dipped in her hand and pulled out tickets.

"What's that?" someone asked.

"These are tickets to the opening, Oscar. Yes, yes, I know who you are. Your sister was in my class last year. You've got the same nose."

"Huh?" Oscar asked.

"Must be a genetic thing. Anyway, darlings, we are going to see the exhibition from Tetzapotitlan. Let's hear you say that one."

Some of the class started to pronounce the city's name, but mostly they butchered it. I didn't even try.

"Don't worry about it," she said, and stood up again. "You've got all term to get your little tongues around everything Aztec. First up, let's hear everything you little darlings know about our South American cousins."

I looked across at Jade who was smiling widely. She winked at me and leaned across.

"Miss Monzote is a nutjob," she whispered. "Totally barmy. It's gonna be great."

I nodded and sank down in my seat a little, turning my head around to see Will in the seat behind me. His eyes were wide and bright and he was totally captivated by the teacher.

"Total nut job," I agreed with Jade.

Chapter Five
Human Sacrifices

AFTER PICKING LUCA up from Power Street Primary School, which was pretty much just across the street from the high school, we walked back down the hill to the lagoon which would take us home. At least, it would take us to the place we were supposed to think of as our home.

For me, 'home' would always be the big old house in Geelong with its wide shady veranda and ceilings that stretched impossibly high. It was home for a long time. I was born in Geelong, and so was Luca. Mum and Dad were together - mostly happy, although even then there was conflict. Mum was always the more ambitious of the two. She always had a 'master plan', while Dad kind of ambled along, deeply engrossed in whatever project he was working on at the time. We had a dog, too. Her name was Molly, although technically she was Molly the Second. She was supposed to be a Corgi-cross but really she was a bitzer this and a bitzer that.

As we walked down the hill towards the pedestrian overpass, Luca pulled out his juice box and offered me some. I thanked him and took a suck, wincing at the luke-warm orange juice before passing it back to him.

"How was your first day?" I asked.

"Fine," he said, probably mocking my standard responses to the same standard question. I decided to change tack.

"What was the third best thing that happened to you today?"

He looked up at me as he sucked on the little straw, his eyes squinting under the sun. I could tell he was seriously thinking back through his day.

"I wasn't killed by a giant seagull," Luca said.

"Huh. Well, that is pretty good," I said, silently wondering what the two best things might have been. I pulled out the Mars bar from my lunch and offered him a bit.

"What's the sixth worst thing that happened to you?" Luca asked me, taking another bite before I pulled it back.

"Sixth?"

He nodded.

"Well, um… the sixth worst thing was …"

There was a *thuk-thuk* sound behind us on the pavement. I looked back and saw a kid on a scooter gliding towards us. Luca and I stopped to let him pass but he skidded to a halt a few feet away and seamlessly walked towards us with the scooter slung over his shoulder.

"Hey there," said Will. He plonked his scooter down and pulled off his helmet, giving Luca a courteous nod before looking at me. "So I was wondering why you never called me."

"What?"

"I figured you weren't being rude, but then I thought maybe I'd done something wrong," he said, running his free hand back through his blonde hair.

"I didn't give you my number," I said, confused. Was he mixing me up with someone else?

He smiled and slapped his forehead.

"That'd be it then," he said. He pulled out his phone and thumb-pressed it on. "So what is it?"

I shook my head. Luca's eyes hadn't left Will's scooter, laying discarded on the pavement.

"Seriously," Will said. "You'll give me your number won't you?"

"Um, no," I said, and took Luca's hand, pulling him along the path. Will grabbed his scooter and hooked the straps of his helmet to his backpack. Then he followed, running a bit to catch up.

"So how was that History lesson?" he said.

"I dunno," I said. "Why are you following me?"

"I'm not following you. I'm going home. This way."

I felt like an idiot but didn't let myself show it. I'd had a lot of experience in consciously overcoming embarrassment through sheer force of will.

"I guess I don't know much about the Aztecs," I said.

"What's to know? Chocolate and human sacrifices. Two of my favourite things. Say, you know what? I'd seriously kill for another bite of your Mars bar."

I rolled my eyes and tossed him the chocolate, enjoying the quick one-two juggle in his hands before he got control of it.

"So what's the sixth worst thing that happened to you?" Luca asked.

"This is Will," I said, savouring the moment. "He's the sixth worst thing."

"Pleased to meet you," Will said. "You wanna hold this for me?"

Will passed Luca his scooter and the kid's eyes almost exploded as his hands curled around the handles. Luca took off ahead of us, swerving deliberately from one side of the path to the other as we moved into the lagoon.

"Do you even know my name?"

"You're Charlene," Will said. "Although, you'd prefer it if I just called you Charlie. Since we'll be going out soon I've decided to call you Charlie. It'll be safer."

"You're dreaming," I said.

"Will be tonight," he shot back. "Seriously, Jade filled me in on you guys. Where've you moved from?"

"The city," I said, evasively.

"Oh right, the 'city'. I guess our town is a bit of a backwater."

I shrugged.

"Nah, fair enough," Will said. "I reckon it'd be hard moving to a new place and a new school. Still, if you want me to show you around, just ask."

He slipped his hand into mine and pulled me along faster. Luca had made it to the road and was looking back at us. I ran with Will, amazed at the way our hands were stuck together - it was mad. I'd never held the hands of someone who wasn't blood-related to me, and it was … I pulled my hand back as we made it to Luca and the three of us looked across to the main street. I could see our place. It wasn't on fire. It looked like it did that morning, so I assumed Dad hadn't blown anything up.

That was a good sign.

"Come on," Will said, guiding Luca and the scooter across the street. "I'll show you some stuff."

"I live that way," I said, gesturing vaguely towards the restaurant.

"Me too," Will said. He was probably lying, but I didn't feel like testing out my theory that he was simply stalking me for more chocolate. He walked on and Luca stumbled after him.

"So what's the best thing to do in this place?" I asked, fully aware that it was a lame question.

We passed the museum. I saw the blue and ivory posters for the Aztec exhibition, but kept walking.

"You know what?" Will said after several steps of thinking. "I think, seriously, that the skate park is the best place. Even if you're not a skater. You're not a skater, right?"

"I'm not a skater," I said.

"That's what I thought."

I wasn't sure if it was an insult, but I wasn't going to pretend to be something I wasn't. At least, I wasn't going to put myself in physical danger to hide the truth. My convoluted (and probably criminal) family history was going to stay hidden though. That was a definite.

"Where is it?" Luca asked.

"Down by the beach. Hey, I'll take you there sometime, little buddy."

"Great," I said and reached for Luca's hand. "But you'd

better give Will back his toy now. We're nearly home."

"Toy?" Luca asked, holding on tight.

"Me too," Will said, taking the scooter from Luca with a warm smile and hooking it over his shoulder like a backpack. "Fact is, this is my place."

He pointed across the street to the police station.

"I don't understand," I said, clearly not lying again. "You're on day release?"

"My dad's the cop," he said with a shrug. "His dad before him was a cop too."

"Are you gonna be a cop?" Luca asked, sounding a little worried. Our family had its prejudices when it came to officers of the law.

"Don't bug him," I said.

"Not sure, yet," Will said, shrugging again. "What about you? You going to follow your mum's path?"

The words stung me and I shied away feeling my cheeks burn. It happens every time, and even though I should have learned how to deal with it by now, I just freeze up. I went to a psychologist, Dr Chrissy, and she helped me, but everything's different in the real world.

"We have to go," I said and walked away, keeping my head down as I dragged Luca along. He didn't seem to care. After waving back to Will, Luca ran his fingers along the shop fronts, leaving little streaks in his wake.

"You think Dad knows the police live across the street?" Luca asked.

I pulled him harder and shoved the key into the lock as we stopped outside the heavy door. I saw Jade washing the inside of the window next door but I forced my eyes away. I yanked open the front door and disappeared up the stairs into the semi-darkness. I felt like the world was coming down around me. There was too much light outside. Too much living. I tried to visualise a rain storm like Dr Chrissy taught me, but all I got was thunderclouds. My lungs heaved in a sack full of air as I sat on the steps, kicking the door closed again. Luca marched up to the apartment, leaving me behind as I tried to pull myself together.

"Charlie!"

My eyes shot open at Luca's cry and I scurried up the steps and into our apartment before he could draw another breath.

The table was still as messy as it was that morning, but one of the chairs had been knocked over. Directly behind the knocked over chair was a dark circle on the wall. A scorch mark.

"Where's Dad?" I asked.

The Reducer was on the carpet but it was lifeless - the power cells were completely drained and there was a black line running the length of the barrel. It must have short-circuited.

Luca held up his hand, his eyes focusing so hard on the little man in his palm that they were going cross-eyed. I stepped closer, bending down to look at the diminutive man. I pushed back my fringe, hooking it behind my ear.

The man stood with his arms crossed, trying to look nonchalant, like this was a very ordinary thing that happened. He was the size of a Lego mini-figure, although his complexion was a bit more in the burnt and blackened variety rather than the usual yellow.

"I guess we're having pizza tonight," I said, picking Dad up by pressing my fingers gently around his waist. I let his dangling legs touch lightly down on the kitchen table before letting him go and he skidded to the surface.

A little sound came from his little mouth but I couldn't understand it.

Luca pressed his fingers around the edge of the table and leaned his chin on the edge, looking down at his father like a predatory dinosaur.

"I think he said we could have ice cream," Luca said.

Chapter Six
Enter the Dragon, Nakaya

IT TOOK AN hour after dinner to get Dad into a jar, because even though he was half the size of my thumb, he wasn't exactly keen on being held in one place. One of the side effects of the Reducer is that while the physical size of a target is reduced, so too is the target's inhibitions and links to modern man. So Dad was acting like Tarzan, beating his chest a bit, and spending a lot of time scratching and being distracted by bright, shiny objects. That's how Luca finally coaxed him into the jar: he used my phone's search light app and some red cellophane to create a tempting light display. My little brother is definitely a Conti - we're all mad scientists here.

With Dad secured for the night, I took Luca back down the stairs so we could get away from the chaos we'd unleashed in trying to catch our miniature father. The sun had slipped away in all the confusion and the street lights had come on, giving us a completely different view of Main Street, Henty Bay. The Cho's restaurant looked magical - light and laughter coming from the painted window, almost like the green dragon was alive and in very good spirits. Across the street, a few other shops were lit up, but closed.

The blue light of the police station reminded me of how close we were to trouble, but I didn't have time to worry, because Luca had pushed his way through a door just past the restaurant.

I rushed after him and opened the door with a clattering of a bell as it pushed inward.

Two women stood just inside what was clearly a kitchy martial arts dojo. Bruce Lee posters covered the wall above the counter and an inflatable sensei bobbed in one corner. Faint, generic music came softly through a radio on the counter, but apart from the two women and Luca, the place was empty.

"Can we sign up?" Luca asked without looking at me. His hand was already scribbling on a form, the pen moving wildly in his fingers. "First lesson is free."

"They always are, kiddo," I said, but then caught the sneers of the two women. Okay, I thought, taken aback by the brazen looks on their faces. It was the first time people of Henty Bay hadn't been super friendly and it hurt me. I don't even know why it hurt, but there it was.

"Can we?"

"Sure," I said. "It's a bit backward, but I guess beggars can't be…"

"Hallo!"

I jumped at the voice, but quickly smiled as a man appeared through a curtain. He was shining like one of those actor-dentists from toothpaste ads. His judo gi was starched white, contrasted with his golden tanned skin, super-bright pearly teeth and a very reflective shaved head.

I felt his presence like a jab to the gut, but in a good kind of way.

"Master Frank, you are always such a surprise," one of the women said. "I think you've given me the hiccups."

"No cure for that, Mrs Park," the Master said. "Unless you want to drink a glass of water upside down…"

"… and backwards," Luca jumped in.

The woman smiled, a little forcedly, and then waved away the Master; taking the opportunity to step outside with her friend. The atmosphere improved immediately, and as the tinkle of the bell swept all memory of the two women from my mind, I found a gi shoved towards me by Master Frank. Luca was already disrobing, t-shirt tossed back over his head and shoes kicked to the side.

"Wait, what?" I said.

"Come on," Master Frank said. "Lesson starts in two minutes. "

"We haven't even signed up," I said. I could smell the bleach from the white uniform, and even though I wanted to stall the crazy instructor, there was something about feeling the hardness of the material under my fingers that brought back happier memories. "We don't have any money."

"First lesson is free," Master Frank said. "Worry about the details later. As my friend Confucius used to say, 'Life is pretty simple really - it is we who insist on making it complicated'. First lesson is free."

Luca pulled up the trousers and yanked at the drawstrings. It was too big for him, but nothing was going to stop him from storming through the curtain which separated the front shop with the back dojo. The whole family used to practice together, back in Melbourne. There was a place in Footscray where we'd go every fortnight, and afterwards we'd wander the streets with kebabs or noodles or whatever else we could find. Dad would be talking too loud, a mountain of a man with his scratchy beard and cheeky-dumb Dad-jokes. And Mum would tolerate him, even though she'd always take him down in practice. Mum would take everyone down. She looked frail, but she was more like a praying mantis than a stick insect. Surgical strikes and no apologies.

Master Frank grabbed my wrist and pulled me through the curtain. The bleach smell was immediately replaced with something more like mothballs and I gagged. On the other side of the curtain the world shifted into something like a demon-infested child care centre. Little kids were running around in white gis, swinging legs and arms in all directions. Older kids were loitering at the edges, arms crossed and dark eyes scanning the room like a bunch of predators.

It was chaos.

And then Master Frank clapped his hands three times as he took his place at the front of the room, and everything fell into place. The kids stopped trying to strangle each other and stood obediently in line, and the older ones shook off their surliness and took up their place behind the little ones. Luca stepped into line at the front as well, giving a blonde kid a fist-tap and a quick smile before turning seriously to the Master.

I adjusted my gi and hid at the back next to a boy I

knew went to the high school. He smiled at me, which was a good sign. He either remembered me and didn't hate me, or he didn't know me at all. The boy bowed his head and then took a kneeling position along with everyone else. I knew the seiza, and so did Luca, and normally we'd sit with students of equal rank but there didn't seem to be much range in this dojo. I felt awkward in a borrowed gi, but there was something reassuring in the ritual.

"Kamiza-ni," called a girl at the front. She wore a brown belt, and apart from Master Frank, she seemed to be the most senior member. "Rei."

"Thank you for coming," Master Frank said as the students' faces turned towards him. "Before we begin warm-ups, I would like to welcome two new students."

I kept my eyes down but I heard Luca say his name when asked, and then I felt everyone's eyes on me. I looked up, trying to look nonchalant.

"And I'm Charlie," I said.

"Excellent," Master Frank said. "Let us begin."

The warm-ups were a bit stiff, in my opinion. Luca was definitely getting into it, though, and jump-squatted like a pro. The little kids seemed to be having a lot of fun, but whenever I caught a glimpse of the older ones I saw boredom in their movements. In the paired warm-up, I matched up against the boy again.

"I'm Colby," he said. "I think we were in Maths together."

Honestly, I couldn't remember exactly where I'd seen him at school. They all kind of looked alike: tanned and blonde. It was like the whole town had been cast from the same genetic shopping list.

"You don't seem to be really into this," I said to him as we practised gripping. He was obviously trying not to squeeze my arm too hard, and he kept laughing nervously. I shifted my feet quickly and pulled backward, flipping him easily to the mat.

I stood up and looked around at the others, still dancing along with the grips. Colby smiled up at me and I took his arm and pulled him up to his feet.

"You're pretty good," he said.

I shrugged.

"Why do you come here?" I asked.

He shrugged.

Master Frank suddenly appeared by my side and Colby managed a fumbled bow.

"My friend says 'it does not matter how slowly you go, as long as you do not stop'," Master Frank said, and Colby stepped back and started to go through some hip twists which made him look even more out of place.

"You have interesting friends," I said. "With interesting sayings."

"Ah, you are too kind. This is Nakaya," Master Frank said. The blonde girl with the brown belt dipped her head slightly, but her eyes never left mine. I'd seen her at school. She was a year older than me, but I was taller. Just. I couldn't help but size her up.

"I'm a State finalist," she said. "Is this your first time?"

"Sure," I said. "First time."

That was enough for her to dismiss me entirely. Master Frank called us to line up again and I stood in the second line so I could keep an eye on Luca who leapt to the front. Nakaya pointed at one of the older kids and as soon as he met her at the front mat, she grabbed his wrists, turned quickly and flipped him hard to the ground. She stepped over his body and pointed at a second student. "Ellicia."

Reluctantly, the next girl stepped up and was immediately grabbed and flipped to the floor.

Luca shot his hand into the air, jumping on the spot.

Nakaya ignored him and pointed at another of the older kids. Master Frank stood silently behind them, unblinking as another student was slammed to the floor. Nakaya took out two more students, and they stayed on the mats, moaning slightly.

I pushed past Colby and the others.

My bare feet felt oddly electric as I walked to face Nakaya at the front of the group. For the second time I could feel every student's eyes on me.

"Mind if I cut in?" I asked, and Nakaya relaxed her hold on her latest victim. The boy blinked and then quickly stepped back, nearly falling over one of the other vanquished students.

"I wasn't going to hurt you this time," Nakaya said. "Unwritten rule. You get one class for free."

I couldn't help but look across at Master Frank who was continuing to ignore the accumulation of tangled teenaged bodies on his mats. For a man who loved his sport, he was doing a terrible job of honouring it.

"Let's go," I said.

Nakaya grabbed my sleeve and pulled me closer, stepping between my legs for a sacrifice take-down. I'd been watching her do the same thing for the past five minutes. She was just as bored as the rest of the students. I grabbed her belt and twisted, shifting my weight and stepping out of her trap. I hooked my leg behind hers and collapsed her easily, landing hard on her back and pinning her to the mat.

I felt her breath shoot out and relaxed my grip, stepping up quickly and to the side, careful not to stumble over the other fallen students. I shot a quick glance towards the Master but he was still apparently in a standing coma.

Nakaya stood up slowly. I noticed for the first time that she had a bow in her hair. Her nails were also incredibly manicured. She didn't look like a girl who ended up slammed to a mat.

"Said it was your first time," Nakaya said, rubbing her

elbow. I could see her working her jaw like some kind of cyborg. "That's not first time luck."

"I'm a liar," I said. "But I don't like bullies."

Nakaya smiled. There was a fierceness there, and pride. If I didn't like the way she threw her authority around, I'd probably be her friend. She reminded me of the kids I hung with back in the city.

We all had to be tough.

"I guess your mum won't be picking you up tonight," Nakaya said and all thoughts of an impossible friendship shattered.

"What?"

The curtain to the dojo parted and Jade came in like a gust of wind, complete with laughter and three shiny red bags. The rest of the students took the interruption as an excuse to go back to their exercises. Jade walked through the white-clad kids like she had done it a thousand times and collected Luca. She ruffled his hair and then turned him towards me, giving me a wide smile. When she stopped right beside me, she noticed the double death stares between Nakaya and me, and lost the smile.

"Saw you guys come in here earlier. What'd I miss?" Jade asked.

"Nothing," I muttered, wondering what Nakaya had meant about my mum.

"A friend of mine once told me there are three paths to wisdom," Master Frank said, materialising beside me again.

"I don't think I want to know," I said.

Master Frank ignored my words. Nakaya folded her

arms in resignation, closing her eyes as Frank spoke.

"First way is through reflection, which is the noblest path. Then there is imitation, which is the easiest. And third, there is experience which is the most bitter of paths."

"What does that even mean?" I asked. "Seriously? These kids are being beaten up by your dragon princess, and you think this is a dojo?"

"Those are words from experience, the most bitter of…"

"I think I'm done here, thank you, sensei," I said. "This town has major problems."

"Every family has problems," Nakaya said. "Like yours, Conti."

I didn't even know she knew my name.

"What problems?" Jade asked, still full of energy, but trying not to look at Master Frank's growing agitation. The man was seriously unhinged. I could see he was about to cry. A very intense, and probably unstable, man.

"Her mum's in prison," Nakaya said with finality and walked off.

I watched her back like it was a moving target dummy at a firing range, and even though my hands didn't move, I counted off the shots I'd put into her cold, heartless body.

"Charlie..?" Luca took my hand and squeezed it. "Can we go now?"

Nakaya didn't even look back. Master Frank sighed as Luca pulled me to the curtains and through to the small shop front on the other side. Outside, I took a deep breath and tried to shake the feeling that this town was full of people who knew too much about my life.

"We have to get home," Luca said, still pulling at me. He seemed desperate to leave, to get me off the street. I let him pull me along, but Jade didn't let me just slip away. She rearranged her shopping bags and fell into step with me.

"So, that was uncalled for," Jade said.

I nodded.

"I mean, like, that's not even true, right? About your mum?" Jade said in that way that sounds like a question but isn't really. My eyes darted to Luca and Jade touched my arm, slowing us down. Luca looked like he was going to cry. His eyes were wide. What did he know?

"She's gone," I said, softly. Jade nodded, let her hand drop and we walked on.

"Um, like…" Jade's voice kind of whined a bit. "When you say 'gone', do you mean she's back in the city? Or, like, she's run away with some hot rock star or something? Or is she, um, you know, dead?"

"What?"

"We're going to be friends, Charlie," she said. "Please don't go weird on me."

"Me going weird? On you?"

"Okay, okay, so maybe I don't have the right way of asking sensitive questions, but I've got three sisters and we're not big on subtleties, okay?"

"No kidding."

"So?"

"So you really want me to answer that?"

"Sorry, but I need to know. You've met my family, you

know my secrets. Is she really in jail? Not that Nakaya ever tells it how it really is, but, that's… you know? That's big."

"She's gone," I said, and moved forward. Jade slipped her hand into mine and squeezed it with compassion, or at least that's what I assumed it was. "Gone," I repeated.

Luca let go of my other hand and ran ahead to the apartment door. He didn't have a key, but he didn't want to stick around either.

"Thanks for telling me," Jade said, whispering into my ear as we walked along. "But, like, do you …. I mean, she's dead, right?"

I pulled my hand away.

"Oh my God, Jade," I said, loud enough for Luca to turn around. "Yes, okay, she's dead. Gone. Not coming back. Ever."

Chapter Seven
Little Problems

SO IT'S BEEN a weird day.

Actually, it's been horrible.

I know you and Dad used to always say every first day is a weird day, but it's different when you're starting high school in a new town. I don't know anyone. All my friends are back in the city, and they probably don't even remember me.

I had to give them false numbers when we left and Dad's deleted my Facebook account again. I'm out of touch.

You might want to know that Dad's got himself shrunk down to the size of a bug again. Luca organised the jar and I punched in the air holes. He's got a bunch of cotton wool at the bottom to make things more comfortable, but he still butted his head against the glass for nearly a whole hour.

I've got the Reducer all disassembled on the kitchen table. I think I know what happened, and it won't surprise you of course, but Dad was playing around with the core inverter and he's got the wires crossed again. It's probably not the only alteration he's made and probably not the only thing that caused the feedback.

But in the end it doesn't really matter, does it? He's

shrunk himself into a mindless mini-man and Luca and I still have to go to school in the morning.

I can hear you telling me to take charge. I'm trying. I really am. I've done the theory, drawn a few plans but I don't have everything to make it work. We're living a million miles from any kind of lab and all I've got is a crooked table for a work bench and a broken ray gun. Even if I could get the energy source to power an external re-router I don't think I can reverse it without killing Dad.

No matter what you think, he's still our Dad.

And he's right here next to me, snoring his itty-bitty head off, probably dreaming of chasing bright lights. He's not going to be able to help. I know that. And, yes, I probably could do this.

One step at a time.

Take charge.

I know.

Why aren't you here?

I don't think I can do this.

Not by myself

I need you Mum.

Dragon ⚡ Princess!

Chapter Eight
The Medusa Reducer

NAKAYA STOOD IN my way like a designer cyclone fence: her immaculate white school shirt and red kilt just that little bit higher quality than everyone else around her. Her shoes were probably polished by professionals and her hair was perfect. How was it even possible for a girl like her to exist? Sure, I could understand a synthetic construct in a lab or an ancient evil spirit taking on such a confident, perky form, but not some girl from Henty Bay.

I noticed her defensive stance, Gwen Stefani brand shoes in line with her slightly turned shoulders. Her smile was what I'd call 'attempted ironic' and her two friends flanked her in the locker corridor.

She wanted a fight.

I turned around and headed back to the courtyard. I might have wanted to go all crazy wildcat on her, but I couldn't afford the attention or the repercussions. Not that I'd lose the fight in physical terms. I could deal with anything Nakaya could throw at me, but a phone call to Dad could have brought in all sorts of unwanted welfare agencies. A trip to the principal's office could be the end of my family's little experiment in normal, everyday living.

"You are such a coward," Nakaya said. Each word shot out like a shuriken, spinning down the corridor and lodging into my back. Thud… thud… thud… "You started this Conti, but I'm going to finish it."

I stopped. My hand pressed down on the glass door, ready to push out into the safety of the courtyard, but I felt those words. I felt the hard, yet clichéd, words. They'd been the words I'd heard my whole life. Everyone wanted a fight.

I heard the Gwen Stefani shoes stopping just behind me. I didn't look back. Ahead of me, through the glass, I could see a group of boys playing games on their phones. And beyond them I could see Miss Monzote talking with one of the senior kids. So close.

"We don't want any ferals like you in Henty Bay."

I dropped my satchel and kicked it to the side lockers, turning back to face Nakaya. She was still ready for a knock-down.

"I don't want to embarrass you," I said.

"You embarrass everyone," Nakaya shot back at me.

"What do you even want? I mean, I don't even think we're

in the same class. Can't you just ignore me like everyone else?"

Nakaya's eyes narrowed, her fists clenched.

And then Will was there.

"What's up?" he asked, pulling off his beanie and tucking it into his back pocket. "You keep messaging me."

"I didn't message you," I said, confused.

"What?" Nakaya's eyes were getting even darker. I was surprised she could see anything - they were like little black holes sucking everything in. "Are you serious?"

And then she laughed.

In that split second I knew that she was an evil abomination, probably a demon, like a real servant of Darkness demon. Her combat stance evaporated and underneath was the spirited, popular perfect student. She slipped her arm around Will's waist and pulled out her phone with her free hand, thumbing through her messages.

"You've been messaging me, silly," she said to Will. "My parentals are going to Melbourne this weekend so we can... oh, Conti, maybe you should go and play with your friends."

"I didn't know you two were married," I said.

Nakaya rolled her eyes. Her two friends stood watching me like statues: dead eyes, frozen mouths. And Will didn't even look at me at all. He was disentangling himself from Nakaya, but smiling the whole time.

I scooped up my satchel and pushed out of there, stepping through the boys playing games on the steps and out into the sunshine.

I fumed for ten minutes, sitting alone on the steps of a classroom portable, flipping the silver cylinder of my Medusa around my fingers, wondering how wrong it would be to throw Nakaya off a cliff. I'd worked out how to do it, but there was still the moral question of whether I should.

I stopped fiddling and examined the Medusa. While Dad was all thumbs when it came to electronics, or pretty much anything really, I had a gift. I'd created a little monster and named it after one of the most misunderstood monsters of all time. Mostly it involved delivering a stunning blast to a person's neurons, preferably delivered as a beam into a target's eyes. There was a bit of memory manipulation and a kind of locked-in experience. Normal girls wouldn't ever think of making such a thing, but I was going through a phase at my last school. Anyway, apart from my growing problems with the inhabitants of Henty Bay I still had to fix my dad and to do that I needed supplies.

The school had a pretty decent science department.

It didn't take a criminal genius to work out the weak spot in the high school lab assistant's schedule. She would take her prac trolley up and down the service elevator fifteen minutes into recess when there was no chance of running into any kids.

The elevator was strictly off-limits to students and staff. There was some problem with insurance coverage, so that meant the only person to use it was the lab tech.

I watched her press her finger into the round button and then moved into position, stepping right behind her like a second shadow. The doors opened and she pushed the silver trolley inside, following it without bothering to look around at me. I was a little more candid, so I gave a final glance over my shoulder and then slipped inside, pulling at the doors as I moved because they were so slow.

"What are you doing?" she asked.

"Trying to... ugh, close the doors."

"Why?"

I managed to secure them in place and turned to look at the woman. It was a rather roomy elevator and we had plenty of space to look each other up and down.

"Are you new?" she asked. "This isn't a place for students."

"It doesn't really matter," I said, and lifted the Medusa up, aiming it level to her eyes. Her pupils tracked it, although she didn't seem the least bit concerned. "In a second, you'll forget all about this."

I pressed the switch and a bright white light shot out into her eyes, shutting down her system like an EMP for humans. Like I said, it was my own invention.

With the lab tech suddenly locked inside her own body, unable to move or even perceive the world around her, I banged the emergency stop button to interrupt our little elevator ride, and hunched down to look at the chemicals lined up along the second row of the trolley. My eyes scanned the labels and I lifted a few of the ingredients I'd need to fix Dad's Reducer and maybe, just maybe, get him back to normal size and normal mentality.

I opened up my satchel and popped the latches on the internal pocket. There was enough space for twelve mini-vials and a stack of bagged compounds. I scrolled through what they had and dropped a bunch of materials into safe and secure compartments. If I rushed it, things could go wrong really quickly. Cracking the glass, releasing some chemicals… I'd be lucky to walk out of there in just a cloud of stink-bomb. More likely I'd be limping out of a smoking crater.

I let out a sigh. My eyes looked up and down the shelves again but there was no real point. It wasn't enough. I wondered why I couldn't have been sent to some kind of military school with military-grade chemicals. Instead, I was stuck scrounging for ingredients in a public school which really had to draw the line at weapons-grade uranium.

"Sorry about the pilfering," I said, stretching my arms a little. It was still recess and I had time to get back to the courtyard where Jade was waiting for me with a bag full of hot potato gems. It was the canteen special.

When the elevator resumed its journey and opened up onto the first floor of the science building, I stepped out and checked we were alone. It was decidedly dead. All of the teachers were probably on yard duty or enjoying a break at their desks. I held the doors open and looked back at the lab tech.

"I really appreciate what you've done for me," I said softly. She looked surprised in her locked-in status. I reminded myself that she wouldn't remember any of the last twenty minutes, and then I aimed the Medusa at her again and pressed the button.

I was gone before she could blink, stepping furiously

down the flight of stairs to the ground floor and then out into the sunshine. I'd only managed to score maybe half of the things I'd need to get my dad back, but half was better than zero.

Three steps out into the yard, I heard the door bang behind me, and the sound blew away any chance I'd had of catching up with Jade. I turned around. There was a boy standing just outside the door wearing a red hoodie, pulled up over his head. It was definitely not school uniform, but I'd seen it before. The other night when I was on the roof I'd seen him, or a boy just like him, riding like a maniac down the main street in the middle of the night.

"You dropped this," he said. He held up his hand, turned it and opened his fist to reveal a small vial of magnesium.

I could feel my jaw clench. A thousand excuses raced through my mind. And then they shot out of my mouth.

"What are you talking about?" I said, altogether too quickly. "Are you insane?"

"Don't think so," he said, and stepped closer, still with the vial offered in the palm of his hand. "Runs in the family though, so probably."

I snatched the vial and carefully slid it into a side pocket of my satchel.

"I suppose you think you're a cop or something," I snapped. Up close he looked to be a year or so older than me. His eyes were brown and didn't seem to blink.

"You need anything else?" he asked, nodding to my bag. Underneath his hoodie, the boy wore the school uniform. I relaxed, a little.

"Sure," I said. "What have you got? Dual component fire retardant epoxy or maybe an icing inhibitor?"

He scratched at his chin and smiled, shrugging a bit.

"Nah, I'm more into grenades, claymores, you know. Maybe pistols, ….. that kind of stuff."

I could tell he was lying.

"You're a real mercenary. That your deal?" I asked.

"Mostly 'Call of Duty'…" he smiled. "Not in your league, princess. But, if you need something, let me know and I can source it."

"Okay, you'll be my 'go-to' guy."

"I'm Dan," he said, holding out his hand.

"Charlie Conti," I said, taking it and giving it a firm shake.

"I know who you are," he said. "Will told me about you."

It took me the rest of the day to shake the feeling that Dan had been watching me. Sitting in my Maths class I stared out the window towards the bike sheds where I'd sat the first day. Had he been one of the skater boys? I didn't know.

When the final bell went, I stashed everything in my locker and happily snapped the padlock shut. I wasn't taking any school stuff home. There was enough for me to do back there without having to worry about finishing my report on Australia's land formations or a Mathsmate homework sheet. For starters, I had to work out how to fix the Reducer and get my father back to the right size.

"See you tonight?" Jade said in a half-question as she walked past, pulling her hair back into a pony tail. She was supposed to be in the restaurant within five minutes of the bell going. "Don't be late."

I smiled and gave a half-hearted wave. There was a school BBQ in three hours: an event to bring the new families together and to showcase the school. It had been made clear to everyone that it wasn't a thing to skip. Jade's entire family were coming. I wondered how much of my own I could manage to wrangle together.

"Can't wait," I said, and slung the mostly-empty satchel over my shoulder. I checked the pocket for my stolen components and ingredients, and then headed out to get Luca.

Little Brother
(rhymes w/ bother)...

Chapter Nine
Brothers And Other Disasters

LUCA SAT ON the carpeted floor playing with packets of hair dye, switching them around like the shell game our Uncle Carl used to play with us. It was harmless enough. While he was entertained, I picked out two packs of flaming red dye and a bleach, and dumped them into my hand basket. There was enough peroxide in them to work, at least in the testing stages. I would probably need more if I was going to move on from the prototype, but my first priority was to get Dad back into a useful size.

"Come on, kid," I said, looking back to my brother who had now taken out the little squirt bottles and started switching them. Blacks into reds, browns into blondes. That couldn't be good. "Luca, oh my God, would you stop trying to get us into trouble?"

I pulled on his arm and yanked him to a standing position.

"You're hurting me," he said.

"Not yet, I'm not…"

I noticed a kid in a hoodie walk past me in the next aisle, and I recognised the hood. It was the mysterious Dan from school. Luca pulled himself away from me while I was distracted and headed towards the front where the old people's products were kept. I had a vision of him riding out on a mobility scooter, but I needed to know whether Dan was going to keep my confidence, especially since I was about to embark upon my sort-of shady experimentation period. I couldn't afford to have the federal police crashing through the apartment door while I was trying to get Dad back to normal.

I was right. It was Dan. He was talking with the pharmacist at the back counter and they looked like they knew each other. A few other customers waited around for 'scripts but I noticed they were keeping their distance from Dan. The pharmacist straightened his spectacles and moved back to his station, behind which lay the cornucopia of prescription medicine. What I'd give for an hour in that store room. It'd make my work a lot easier, but there was too much risk of being caught.

"Hi," I said brightly, poking Dan in the back as I came up to him. He hadn't seen me, obviously, because he shrunk away at the touch, turning around with such a look of terror on his face. His eyes shot up and down, taking me in from pathetic runners to the embarrassment of my red face. And in an instant I knew I'd done the wrong thing, and I felt terrible. "Sorry," I said, softly, but his eyes were looking behind me, scanning the store, moving like lightning.

It was scary weird.

"It's just me," I said and quickly picked up a bag of glucose jelly beans from the counter. "Just dropped in to get me some red jelly beans, you know? For studying … and … stuff."

Dan's face hardened, like he was angry with me for even talking to him. What was it with the boys of Henty Bay? Or maybe it was me? The pharmacist ambled back with a genial smile on his face and handed over a small box of tablets, slipping Dan a 'script as he did. Dan gave him a nod and then shoved them into the front pocket of his hoodie, pushing past me as he bolted for the door.

"You can pay for the jellies at the front," the pharmacist said, smiling still. "And I think you'd look lovely with red hair. Good on you, for being so brazen." He went back to his checklists, leaving me feeling five shades more furious than brazen.

"Oh no, I don't think so," I said and left the jelly beans on the counter, slamming them down just a little too hard. "That's way too much rude for today."

I stormed down the aisle, stepping over the hair dye Luca had been playing with, and caught up with Dan as he stepped out on to the street.

"Hey," I called out, but he didn't stop like I'd expected. "I said 'hey', gangster." Still, he didn't stop, so I had to run ahead of him, cutting him off as we stood outside the supermarket. Dan was still angry with me for some reason, his shaded face obscured by the hood. I realised I was still carrying the plastic shopping basket with the boxes of hair dye and felt a pang of dread as I imagined store detectives descending upon me and dragging me off to juvie. I knew I had to act fast.

"What do you want?"

"I want to know why you are such a jerk," I shot back at him.

"You'll find out."

"Well," I said, not exactly sure of where I was headed. "Maybe I'll find out now, because you'll tell me. Now, as in at this very moment."

"I don't like people."

Fair enough, I thought. I was heading in that particular direction myself after what had happened with Will. I thought I had it all figured out. Things were falling into place, but then weirdness had to creep back into my life.

"I'm not people," I said. "Seriously, you know that. What's going on with you?"

I couldn't help it, but my gaze dropped to his pocket and we both knew I was wondering about the packet of meds.

"Nothing is going on with me," he said slowly; probably too slowly, like he was clenching his jaw way too hard. "I have to get home."

"Yeah, well, I have to buy this hair stuff or I'm going to jail, but you need to relax a bit. You can't just hate at me like that. You're my 'go to guy', remember? What if I have to 'go to' and you treat me like you don't even know me?"

Dan shrugged a little, but the hate was slipping away. He started to say something but clammed up again.

"I need to know you've got my back," I said. "In case I have to go black ops, you know?"

He smiled then.

"That's stupid," he said.

"No, that hood is stupid," I said.

I reached out and pushed back his hood, letting the light onto his face. He flinched a bit and I noticed his left eye had a shiner from where he'd been hit by something, or someone. The side of his head had a shaved lightning bolt symbol and he had a kind of faux-hawk thing happening.

"Wow, impressive head under that hood," I said, smiling.

"Okay, fair call, I'm sorry," he said. "I have to get back to my mum. She needs these pills or things will be bad for a month. It's not conspiracy, I just hate this town."

"…said every kid ever," I added.

"You've got company," Dan said, raising his eyebrows and jutting his chin.

"I'm busted, aren't I?"

"See you later," he said with a smile and then shucked his hood up again and sauntered over to his bike which was chained up. It was probably the same bike I'd seen on the first night in Henty Bay, and things started to fall together.

"Excuse me," a voice said behind me.

"Yeah, look, sorry," I said, turning around. "I wasn't stealing this stuff."

The girl was beautiful. She obviously worked at the make-up counter inside. She gave me an easy smile and waved my worry away.

"No, of course not, but you need to get your little brother. He's got a sultana stuck up his nose."

You'd think that having to hold your brother while the piercing specialist used thin forceps to pull a sultana out of his nose would be the worst thing possible, right? Unfortunately, my day was a landslide of unfortunate events. At school, the whole thing with Nakaya and Will was still haunting me, plus my nearly compromised criminal activities after having to temporarily paralyse a lab technician... well, it could have worked out better. After extricating the sultana from Luca's nose and paying for the hair dye and a bunch of aspirin ("You should lie down, dear. And drink lots of fluids."), we went to the supermarket.

It was a bad move.

I should have known better.

You hear that all the time, I know, but I needed to complete my shopping. Without the absorbing qualities of sodium polyacrylate or some other substitute I'd be just hacking around the core problem. I needed to get my Dad back to normal size.

I tried to buy nappies. They are super-absorbent - it says so on the packet; but as I pushed Luca around in the trolley I noticed that we were drawing a lot of attention. I recognised a lady from the chemist who seemed especially disappointed in my big sister duties. We found the baby aisle and I started to compare the ingredients of nappies.

The 36 pack seemed my best choice. Given the probable percentage of absorbent crystals inside the disposable nappies I'd need at least a couple dozen. I dropped the box into the trolley just as the Walrus strolled past the end of the aisle and casually looked down at me. He stopped. Of course.

"Good afternoon Charlene," he said, still not forgiving me for being listed as absent in his first class. His bushy eyebrows were arched and his bushy walrus-beard seemed to be trembling as he looked at the box of nappies.

"Hi Mr.... uh..." I had forgotten his name and didn't think teachers would appreciate their students using nicknames. "Oh Luca, you silly brat."

I put my hands on my hips like Mum used to do (all the time) and shook my head. Luca fell into his role immediately.

"Sorry," he said.

I lifted the box out of the trolley and put it back on the shelf.

"We don't need nappies, silly. You're a big boy now."

"I am such an idiot," Luca said, slapping his forehead.

We confused the Walrus and he moved on, a little unsteadily as he tried to work out whether I was insane. I needed the crystals but I really couldn't risk people thinking we had a baby stashed at home under the floorboards, or worse. What if they thought I was some kind of teenage mum?

I needed a plan B and as I pushed my trolley into the next aisle I mentally slapped myself for not thinking of it sooner. We didn't need nappies for our phantom baby, we just needed clumping clay kitty litter for our non-existent cat. Sodium bentonite would work just as well to absorb liquid. Luca thought it was a stroke of genius and started thinking up cat names in case we were cross-examined by any of my other teachers.

"Sparkles," he said. "Or Trevor."

"Hang on," I said, looking at the crazy number of brands available. It took up half of the aisle and all I really saw was a blur of colour and cat faces.

"Get that one," Luca said as he scrambled out of the trolley and went to play with the dog toys. "It's Trevor's favourite."

"Alley Cat Kitty Litter?"

"Sure," he said, dismissing the conversation as he started to swing the different metal dog leads into each other, tangling them horribly.

Alley Cat used to be a hard-core vigilante in the 1990s. As I scanned the back of the 1kg pack of Alley Cat Kitty Litter I wondered how he'd view his legacy. His three claw 'scratch' logo was emblazoned on the front of the pack. The same 'scratch' had filled criminals with terror, but now it was supposed to bring confidence to cat owners. I shrugged and dumped it into the trolley, satisfied it contained enough sodium bentonite for my purposes. Besides, it was on special. I dropped another three bags into the trolley and looked around for Luca, half expecting him to be in deep conversation with one of my teachers. He was still pulling on the dog leads and treats, testing their tensile strength, stifling a yawn. He looked bored, and that was never a good look on him.

"Nearly done," I said.

He squeaked a chew-toy and raised his eyebrows at me like he didn't believe it.

"Come on. You want Dad back, right?"

Luca shrugged and dropped the toy. "I guess."

"Well, he's not going to suddenly pop back into Dad-size by himself. I need some stuff, and I couldn't get everything today at school."

"Do you think we could get a pug?"

"Huh?"

"You know, a pug," Luca said. "Maybe we could buy one now, when Dad's … you know … happy."

"No," I said, pushing the trolley along the aisle. "I think that's a very bad idea. Besides, don't they have breathing problems?"

Luca jumped onto the end of the trolley and rode it lazily, leaning his head on his crossed arms. I could tell he was day-dreaming about smashed-in dog faces, and as we turned into the next aisle I almost ran over Momma Cho and one of her daughters. I pulled the trolley up and dislodged Luca, right into her arms. There was a split-second when time seemed to stop. Momma Cho's face was all wide-eyes and twisted lips. Luca seemed to freeze again, caught in the landlady's grip.

And then the woman laughed. She squeezed Luca closer and gave him a peck on the cheek, looking across to me as he squirmed himself free and slipped past the daughter, who looked like she was pregnant.

"What you doing here?" Momma Cho asked. "Cook out tonight. You should be getting ready like Jade."

"Oh, right, the barbecue," I mumbled. "Not sure we're going."

"Nonsense."

"Dad's a little sick," I said, my voice becoming a little clearer as I weaved my lie. "He gets headaches."

Momma Cho waved away my fib. The daughter rolled her eyes, just like Jade would have done. She had the same willowy figure but she was older, maybe twenty years old. And the round ball of her belly was so perfect, I couldn't really take my eyes off it. Jade never said anything about her sisters, except for the usual dismissive insults.

"You come with us," Momma Cho declared.

"To the barbecue?" I wasn't sure how to say no, and Luca had made his way to the end of the aisle. "It's okay if I miss it."

"Don't be silly girl. You come with us."

She patted me on the arm as she swept past, picking up some sauces and passing them back to the daughter.

"See you later," the daughter said.

"Wait," Momma Cho said, turning back. "You have cat?"

"Yes," Luca said, jumping back onto the front of the trolley.

I shook my head vigorously, clamping my hand over Luca's mouth, hoping he wouldn't chomp down on my fingers.

"No cat, Mrs Cho," I said. "It's for a science experiment."

"Hmm," she grunted with a fierce nod of her head. "Cats no good. Kill all the beautiful birds. Better to have girls than cats."

"See you later," Jade's sister said again, and guided her mother back to their shopping.

I slapped my hand lightly across the top of Luca's head and he started laughing.

Chapter Nine and a Half
Where's Dad?

BACK AT THE apartment we quickly realised Dad was gone when we saw the broken jar on the kitchen floor. After an hour of searching we still hadn't found him. Luca even climbed through the man hole cover in the bathroom but all he found in the attic were spider-webs and the distinct smell of possum pee.

I stacked the bags of kitty litter and the boxes of nappies I'd decided to go back and get, just in case. Then I sat at the table and rolled the barrel of the Reducer around, thinking of ways to boost the capacity without overloading everything again. I'd also toyed with the idea of attaching the Medusa to the barrel for a kick-ass firearm, the one and only, Medusa-Reducer.

There was a quick rap on the door and Jade poked her head inside, eyes wide as she took in the kitty litter. I slipped the Reducer into my pocket and stood up, casually dropping my school jumper over the rest of my deconstructed supervillain weaponry.

"You have a cat?" Jade asked.

"No."

"A baby?"

I shook my head and totally ignored the mounting evidence in the room. Luca came out of the bathroom holding one of Dad's old minion masks, but did a complete 180 and disappeared again before Jade could see him. She was normal Jade, all smiles and full of friend-energy. I still didn't know why she was bothering with me.

"So mum's adopting you for the night," Jade said, giving up the inquiry. She was wearing a sheer black singlet over a black crop top and designer jeans. In her hands she carried two plastic bags of hot, sweet smelling take-out. "Said you should give this soup to your dad. It's something to help his head. Usually does the trick for our dad, but probably not drinking a slab every night would also help with that."

"Huh?" I said, looking down at my own shirt which looked generic. I needed to buy new clothes.

"Kidding," she said. "Ready for the barbie?"

"Can we eat now?" Luca said, as he returned from the bathroom. He eyed the plastic bags like a wolf, but I snatched them away from him.

"They're for Dad," I said. "Thanks Jade."

Luca opened the fridge door with a groan.

"Your fridge is pretty bare, Goldilocks," Jade said. "Come on, let's get to the barbecue before that little boy dies of starvation."

"You really think it's that important?" I asked. "I mean, I've been to a few schools and they're all pretty much the same. They won't miss me. Hardly any of the teachers even know who I am."

Jade waved away my concerns.

"It's not about the teachers, Charles. It's a chance to hang with your new best friend."

"Please don't call me Charles," I said. "Can I get changed or something? Luca and I only just got home."

"Yeah, sure. Little brother and I can catch up on gossip while you're at it, like why you and Dan Galkin were seen exchanging smolderingly hot looks in the street this afternoon."

"No idea what you mean." Luca closed the fridge, then slumped at the table, looking hungry and bored. "Charlie doesn't exchange looks with boys."

"You're right, we should feed him," I said, panicking. "I'll just go in this."

Jade's lips twisted with disapproval but didn't say anything. I pulled my hair back into a ponytail and gave one last glance behind me at the door, hoping to see a miniature near-naked man on the table, smiling and waving me goodbye.

But Dad was still gone.

Chapter Ten

The Henty Bay Secondary College Family Barbecue

W E WALKED THE long way to school, over the bridge which spanned the highway, but before we left, Jade assembled the Chos. Her parents fussed over Josie, Jade's older sister who was twenty weeks pregnant and conspicuously without a partner. Luca helped out by holding handbags as the Cho women made final preparations on the street.

I used the time to wander across to the police station. I saw Will's scooter leaning against the brick building, his sleek helmet hanging on the handles. I looked back to Luca and the Chos but they were arguing about Josie's shoes. Flats or heels? It seemed to be a serious predicament.

While they tried to convince Josie to ditch the heels, I pulled out the Reducer and tapped it against my thigh, weighing up scientific research against 'the right thing to do'. It needed some field tests and Will really loved his scooter. I could see him with Nakaya, all hands on and practically entwined with each other, and I felt the rise of scientific research boil in my veins.

I raised the Reducer and pressed the button. The scooter

trembled slightly and then seemed to fold in on itself, reduced, in an instant, to the size of a Bratz Doll accessory. Satisfaction swept through me. I bent down and picked up the scooter, lifting it up and marvelling at the detail. The helmet was unaffected.

"Conti!" Jade yelled. "Come on!"

I slipped the Reducer back into my pocket and caught up with my brother and the Chos. My hand was closed around the incriminating evidence, but somewhere between the bridge and the school, I got rid of it.

The satisfaction remained though.

The Henty Bay Secondary College Family Barbecue was as exciting as you'd expect it to be. Teachers were lined up behind an enormous barbecue, turning fat sausages while chatting with eager parents. Other teachers mingled with other parents around plastic chairs and tables, and all the kids hung far back around the tree-line. Most kids had dressed up in their best casual clothes, but a few were still wearing uniforms so I didn't feel completely ruined.

Luca sat next to me with a plastic cup full of orange cordial and a plate with two fat sausages wrapped in white bread and layered with tomato sauce. He was stuffing them into his face like a professional, and next to him was a little black-haired boy he knew from school. They were talking tactics for Skylanders.

Jade and Josie, were sitting with me against a crooked tree. I took a bite out of a vegie burger, trying to imagine it didn't taste like cardboard. I hadn't seen Will yet, but Jade had already said he was coming. I imagined he'd arrive with Nakaya's family.

"You're a bit moody," Josie said to me, kicking me in a friendly way. She was sitting on a low hanging branch, like a bench, swinging her legs next to where Jade and I sat. "Aren't these supposed to be the best years of your life?"

"I don't think that's ever true," Jade said.

"Seriously, why're you so quiet, Charlie?"

"Her dad's sick," Jade said. "No biggie."

"No, it's fine. I'm fine," I said. "I guess moving to a new town is a bit tougher than I thought. But you guys have been great."

"Are the girls giving you a hard time?" Josie asked.

I shrugged. It was more about Will giving me a hard time, but I didn't want to say anything. Jade finished her sausage and wiped her fingers on the napkin, one finger at a time. I smiled.

"Nothing out of the ordinary," I said, as I wrapped up what was left of my vegie burger, hoping no one would notice I didn't eat it.

"Nakaya's on her case a bit," Jade said. "But that's because Charlie is totally kick-ass when it comes to judo."

"What about those horrible Year 9 girls?" Josie asked.

"I don't think I've met them," I said, but I noticed Jade had gone really quiet. She pulled up her legs and rested her chin on her knees. She had really long legs, like a model. "But I'll keep an eye out for them."

"Yeah, they're trouble," Josie said. "Gave Jade a hard time. Don't give them any opening, okay?"

"Um, sure. I guess," I said, and then I saw Will. "Oh no…"

I didn't realise I said it out loud, but the combination of talking with Josie about girls I didn't know, worrying about

Jade getting a bit melancholy, and the sudden appearance of Will and his dad walking towards us made me lose my train of thought.

"'Oh no'?" Josie asked, and then sighed. "Here comes the Sheriff. Hi Will."

Will nodded hello to Josie and then held out a cup of cordial to me. I noticed he had three sausages wedged under his arm, wrapped up in napkins but still oozing a little sauce.

"I found you," he said.

"We're always in this tree," Jade said. "It's the Cho Tree."

"Yeah, I think he meant Charlie," Josie said, and started to disengage herself from her trunk-seat. Will's dad helped her down and she gave her pregnant belly a little rub before brushing leaves from her bottom. "Thanks Sergeant Chase."

"You be careful, Josie," the man said. I remembered that Will's dad was a policeman. He wasn't in uniform, but there was something very policeman-like about his moustache and general bulkiness of frame. He didn't look like Will at all.

"I'm always careful," Josie said, and sighed as she noticed her mother bailing up one of the Maths teachers. "I better go and rescue Miss Fleming."

"Are your mum and dad here?" Will's dad asked me.

"It's Charlie," Will said, helpfully.

"No, um, Dad's not feeling well."

"Maybe we'll meet another time then," Sergeant Chase said. "I haven't had the chance to meet either of them yet, but it's a small town, as you probably know, right? We'll bump into each other soon enough."

I managed a weak smile, and then Will's dad moved

on, leaving us awkwardly standing in front of each other.

"So, you know that thing with Nakaya…" Will said, giving away any chance of ignoring the problem.

"Thing?" Jade said. Somehow I'd forgotten she was there, but sure enough, Jade came right up to me and slung her arm over my shoulder. "Nakaya deserved it, Will. Don't come and defend your girlfriend."

"Girlfriend?" I said, even as Will said the same thing. There was a weird moment, but the confused look in Will's eyes was worth it. I'm a quick study, and the word took him by surprise.

"No, that's what I mean," Will said, struggling to untangle the three sausages under his arm. He held them out and Jade took one with a firm nod. "Um, I don't know what was happening back there, but you disappeared…"

"You were planning a date," I said. He held out the sausage but I didn't take it.

"No I wasn't."

"Yeah, you were. You two were messaging."

"Really?" asked Jade, mouth half filled with bread, meat and sauce.

"No, like, that's not what was happening." He held the sausage out further. "I got this for you."

I narrowed my eyes at him.

"I'm a vegetarian."

"But you eat chocolate," he said.

"Yeah, it's a vegetable."

He smiled and I wondered how intelligent he really was.

"Right," Jade said. "This is awkward."

"Um, look, Nakaya is my tutor. She's helping me with

piano lessons, which are really dumb, I know, but my dad really wants me to do them because his dad did them and …. you know."

"Nakaya is your piano teacher?" I asked. Of course, Nakaya could play the piano. She was probably a pro-tennis player, ballerina and avant-garde painter as well.

"Yeah, it's not … are you really a vegetarian?"

"She stopped eating animals when she was seven," Luca said. His friend had gone and he was biting the edges of his plastic cup. "But I'm a carnivore. It's okay." Luca took the sausage and shoved it into his mouth, chomping happily as he watched Will, probably checking out if there was any more concealed food.

"So you weren't going on a date?" I asked.

"No," Will said, smiling and biting the last sausage. "Well, not with Nakaya. I wanted to ask you to come and check out the Skate Park."

"Skate Park?!" Luca shouted, jumping to his feet. "Totally, yes!"

"You're asking me out on a date to a Skate Park?" I asked.

"Well, not a date-date, obviously. But you should check it out on the weekend. Gonna be a great day and I can show you some stuff."

"Sure," Jade said, sounding bored. "She'll be there."

"Cool," Will said, and somehow managed to eat the rest of the sausage in one bite. "See you at twelve. Saturday."

The Sixth Worst Thing...

Chapter Eleven
Charlie Conti, Trainee Waitress

SITTING AT THE kitchen table, forearms encrusted with kitty litter crystals and tufts of lining from disemboweled disposable nappies, I found myself thinking about Will Chase and how he was some kind of weird perfect mix of cute boy and naive village idiot. Mum always said the ones you had to watch out for were the dopey, good looking ones. Of course, I never had to even think about it before because given our always-on-the-move living arrangements, coupled with fairly regular life and death situations, I'd never really given myself a chance to think about boys. You know, like that.

But I was fourteen now. And I was at a pretty ordinary school, in a pretty ordinary bayside town, with a pretty ordinary profile if you ignored the run-ins with local psychopaths like Nakaya and small-time crims like Dan.

I looked at the Medusa-Reducer, propped up on a weapon stand we'd picked up from one of Pearl Zhang's clearance sales back in Melbourne. It was around the time Dad decided he was going to try being a double-agent, which failed miserably. I wiped my hands on the wet dish cloth which hung over my shoulder and stood up. Dad was still gone, but when I got him back I now knew I had the means to return him to his normal, dopey giant self.

Part of me didn't want him back. When I looked out the window I saw the police station and I knew that if I wanted anything to happen with Will, and seriously, I didn't even know what I wanted there, but if I wanted anything even remotely normal to go down, I couldn't have Dad around. He was hopeless.

"Yes!" shouted Luca from the bedroom. "Totally burned!"

I left the window and went to see what he was up to. Given the way he was rolling across the bed with a console controller in his hand, eyes somehow locked to the 32" screen of the TV even though he was squirming like a lizard, I figured he'd aced another level of his computer game.

"You know you're not supposed to hijack cars, right?" I said.

He ignored me and kept running down the virtual street, firing off shots at cars and street lights. I was a bit worried about the kinds of games kids were into these days, but then I caught myself and remembered that Luca had been involved in real street battles before he could walk. Dad had him slung across his back on one heist, guns a'blazing.

For a family of supposed evil geniuses, we sure had our fair share of idiots.

"Hey, kiddo, I'm going to go help the Chos, okay? Jade wasn't at school today, so they need some extra help."

Luca twisted his hands, swerving the console around an imaginary obstacle.

"If you don't answer me, I'm gonna take the computer thing back to Jade's house."

"I heard you, I heard you," Luca said, poking his tongue a little through his white teeth: all concentration and eight year old determination. "I'll be okay up here."

"I'm only working for, like, two hours at most. And I'll bring you some stuff to eat when I'm done, right?"

"Ten four on that, Mother Bird," he said.

"Yeah, I'm going to ignore that. And don't touch the Medusa-Reducer. It's on the table. Do not mess with it. Serious face, here, okay?"

"I heard you. Jeez."

I winced and stepped back, closing the door on his virtual world. The kitchen was full of torn kitty litter bags and there were two piles of empty nappy boxes. Throughout the room there was a faint smell of cats. Totally in my head, I know, but with all the kitty crystals and the general mess it looked like we should have a whole army of cats living here.

I dropped the wet dish cloth on the table and pulled

the protective black plastic sheets over the gun and its stand. Normal Conti house, but it was time to go down and start working at a 'real person' job. I shrugged out of my school jumper and gave my white shirt a quick once-over to make sure it looked presentable enough. Once I'd figured out how to get Dad back I was definitely going to need to go clothes shopping.

"It'll do," I said to myself.

And then I let myself out of the apartment.

The restaurant was actually busy. It didn't look like it from the outside, but once I'd pushed the door open I was greeted by buzzing conversations, laughter and upbeat music piping through hidden speakers. Jade's sister, Juliet, took my arm as soon as my eyes adjusted to the dim lighting and turned me towards the back. She was in Year 12 and was the smartest Cho girl. Almost as smart as a son, Momma Cho had bragged. She had long hair, like Jade, wore glasses and was an expert multi-tasker.

"You're in the kitchen, champ," she said. "Stage one of indoctrination starts with stuffing spring rolls and listening to Ma's stories of the Old Country."

"Sounds great," I said. Juliet laughed and gave me another little shove, letting me find my way through the tables to the back. I passed two families and one of my teachers. It was Miss Monzote, the History teacher. She was reading a newspaper, all sprawled out on the table like old people did. Her hair was hanging like black curtains either side of her face and her eyes were drinking up the news stories. She looked amazing. Her thin arms were bent at the elbows, decorated with rings of gold at her wrists, and in one of her hands she held a wine glass. The woman had style.

"Charlie, c'mon," Jade hissed at me from the open kitchen door. "You're late."

"I thought you were sick," I said, hurrying the last few steps before she pulled me into the kitchen, letting the door close behind me. As soon as I stepped inside I was overwhelmed by the smells of Cho's restaurant kitchen. It was amazing, like a big warm hug from your favourite aunt - if your favourite aunt was made of sweet and sour pork.

"Late is late," Jade hissed again, turning me around and tying a white apron to my waist. She pulled tightly and I yelped.

"Five minutes," I hissed back. "Why are you in such a bad mood?"

"I'm not."

"You nearly cut me in half with the apron, Jade."

She bit her lip and lowered her eyes. Something was bothering her, but it wasn't going to come out anytime soon. Momma Cho swung a knife in my direction, levelling it at my eyes from across a work bench.

"Hullo Sharlie, girl," she said. "Welcome to your first day of working."

She nodded at a bowl of shoots and chopped cabbage and then waved the knife like a wand at sheets of thin, almost transparent pastry.

"You do the rolling," she snapped.

"I can do that, Mrs Cho."

"After the washing of hands," Momma Cho snapped again, waving the knife in the direction of a sink. Jade already had the water running and I dipped my hands under the stream, rubbing with soap to get rid of any last trace of kitty litter from my hands.

"So this is work experience," I said, trying to capture the feeling of being a normal girl.

"This is my life," Jade said, sadly.

She showed me how to stuff spring rolls and plate up gong bao chicken, all the time talking about school and Josie's baby and TV shows and the problems of being a Chinese daughter. She skirted around why she hadn't been in school but I figured I could sense a trap when I saw one. I tried to be sympathetic, but getting my hands literally stuck into a Chinese menu had me in normal girl overdrive.

"You girls take over out front," Momma Cho called out through a jet of steam that shot up from a huge pressure cooker. "Too much blah-blah-blah out here. You go help sisters."

"You mean I get to be a waitress?" I asked.

"Take food out, smile, bring empty plates back here."

"Oh my God, this is fantastic."

"Try and be a little less enthusiastic, Charlie," Jade said. "You're not getting paid for this, you know."

I waved away her concerns and pushed out into the restaurant, which had filled up even more since I'd arrived. Jade bumped into me and we looked around, trying to get our bearings. Josie was still at the front of the restaurant, and Juliet was explaining menu items to a couple of women wearing cat cardigans. Most people were already eating, but we spotted a young couple who had only just taken their seats.

"I'll get them," Jade said quickly. "You take your time or you'll get a nose bleed."

I walked to the front, smiling at the patrons as I past. I spotted Miss Monzote's table again and she had a guest. The newspaper was gone, and in its place was a low lying dish and three blue satin bags, like jewellery bags. A man sat opposite her, and while she was still as poised and sophisticated as ever, surprisingly, the man had wild grey hair, a messy beard and a thick dark brown coat. He looked like a dodgy uncle.

And the man was making all kinds of noises, getting stuck into a bowl of wontons and a side of spring rolls. His hands were moving all the time, wolfing it down. Miss Monzote, on the other hand, sat quietly with her half glass of red wine.

She noticed me and smiled, tilting the glass in my direction. I returned the smile and stopped at their table looking to see if I could take away any empty plates.

Everything looked half-full. I was a bit confused.

"Aren't you a little young to be working?" the teacher asked. The flash of gold from her wrists was almost deliberate. The man stopped eating and looked up.

"I'm not really working," I said. "Just helping out."

"Well, you're a good example for others, Miss Conti. I'm sure you'll get a lot out of our excursion next week."

"Excursion?" the man asked.

I smiled, trying not to look at the strip of wonton hanging out of his mouth. The man looked like he was in his fifties, maybe older, but he didn't look like a Monzote.

"The children and I will be visiting the Chalchiuhtlicue exhibition."

I could tell the man didn't catch the name of the exhibition any more than I did. The exotic word fell from Miss Monzote's lips like melted chocolate. I wished I could say it with even half as much grace.

"The Aztec thing," Miss Monzote said with a tinkling of laughter, waving her hand at her guest, playfully tapping the hand that held his chopsticks. "I told you before."

He nodded, but still looked confused. Miss Monzote's free hand touched one of the satin bags and pulled it closer to her side of the table. The man smirked, one side of his mouth twisted upward. He reached out his hand and pulled one of the other bags closer to him.

"You silly little man," Miss Monzote said, tapping his hand again. "Miss Conti will think the two of us are such squabbling children."

I had no idea what was happening. Part of me hoped it wasn't some weird internet hook-up thing, but I didn't have to worry too much because Josie waved me over to the front of the restaurant and I quickly smiled my exit from the teacher and her companion. Grown ups were so strange.

Josie's back was playing up so I stepped in to help her out, letting her take a seat at the front desk. She could still direct customers, but I helped out too, guiding people to tables and thanking those who had finished. Somehow I kept managing to walk past Miss Monzote and the bearded man. The bags contained gold, I was sure of that. I even caught a glimpse of it as I set down dishes on the next table over, and they were talking wildly about the Aztec exhibition.

I tried not to eavesdrop, I really did; but when you've been raised around minions and two-bit super-criminals, it's a hard habit to break. There was an envelope sitting between the grizzled old man and Miss Monzote, and it was probably full of dirty money. It seemed so old school. The flat plate thing, which sort of looked like a vase but not quite, was a bit too out of place to ignore. Miss Monazite kept touching it but didn't seem to like it as much as the man wanted her to.

"Will this hold it?" Miss Monzote asked, running a finger down its side.

The bearded man shrugged and took another drink of the beer in his hand.

"This is genuine late classic Aztec, around 700AD."

"That's not the right period."

"Close enough. They won't know the difference."

"She will know," Miss Monzote said. "It's totally wrong, Gerhardt. You promised me an Olmec period vase."

I smiled, knowing that I had been right about it being a vase. I was pretty good at surveillance. The man shrugged again and stirred his chopsticks around what was left of the wontons.

"A vase is a vase, Fraulein. You spend too much time worrying about the little details and you'll miss the big event."

He leaned forward and sniffed.

"That's a pretty necklace you've got there."

Miss Monzote's hand went protectively to her neck, her fingers encircling the tortoise amulet. I'd noticed it in History class too. It was very thick and not at all what you'd expect a fine fashionista like Miss Monzote to be wearing. I'd imagine some kind of ankh or an ancient diamond around her neck, not some clunky reptile stone.

"This is not for sale," Miss Monzote said slowly. Her eyes flicked towards me and her lips pursed slightly. "And we are done speaking about this."

I smiled quickly and scooped up the empty plates from the next table, dropping a pair of chopsticks as I hurried. Jade appeared next to me and picked up the sticks. Her eyes were red and she looked terrible. Maybe she was still sick.

"Mum says you'd make a better daughter than me," Jade said softly as she filled up the napkin dispenser on the table, deliberately not looking at Miss Monzote and her guest. "But if she sees you eavesdropping like that, you'll be just another disappointment. Shake it up, Conti."

"I'm not…"

"…eavesdropping?" Jade laughed bitterly, and patted me on the shoulder. "Right."

I stacked the plates, clanking them in a professional way, and marched past Jade. I could hear her talking with customers as I pushed through the swinging doors and into the kitchen. She was right, of course. I was supposed to be working at the restaurant, not taking my imagination for a walk.

"Good girl," Momma Cho called as I dropped off the plates. "You tell Jade to stop playing on phone."

"Ah, okay," I said. I had seen Jade checking her messages all night. Didn't really worry me, but it probably wasn't the right thing to be doing on a work night. I figured I might drop a little sarcastic comment next time we passed each other. Eavesdropping wasn't the worst crime, apparently. Of course, when I did pass Jade again and made a comment about keeping her phone in her pants, I didn't expect Jade to start crying.

Tears just burst out of her eyes. No sound. No action. Just rolling water.

She bolted for the kitchen and I headed to the front desk. Josie was chatting with some customers, one of whom seemed to be an old school friend of hers because they were talking about Miss Monzote. I looked at the teacher's table but she had gone. When the customers left, I leaned close to Josie, looking at the bookings.

"Are you okay, Conti?"

"Sure, sure," I said, looking for the teacher's name. "Did Miss Monzote book a table tonight?"

"No, she's a walk-in. We don't actually have to book many tables. Why do you want to know?"

"Just wondering about her friend."

"Interested in starting rumours or stopping them?" Josie asked.

"Duh, I'm not like that. I was just interested, that's all."

Josie was right, though. What could I possibly do with the information? It's not like I was actually interested in Miss

Monzote as a person, and did it really matter who she saw outside of the classroom? She was entitled to a life, right?

"Professional standards, Conti. What happens in the restaurant, stays in the restaurant."

"That's a no-brainer, Josie. I wouldn't spread stuff. I know how bad that can be, trust me," I said.

"Yeah, well, Jade's one to talk to about that," Josie said, pulling out a register receipt and squinting at the numbers. "Gotta check this receipt for table 19. They said they only had the chow mein. Remember?"

I shook my head.

"That was one of Jade's tables, I think. Um, Is Jade okay?" I asked Josie as we looked over the receipt together. "I mean, she's been kind of snappy tonight."

Josie shrugged and picked up her reading glasses, slipping them on to get a better view of the totals.

"Mum isn't really happy with her homework," Josie said. "Thinks she should do more. Usual thing."

"But we've only just started the school year. There isn't any real homework yet."

"See, our mother doesn't think like that," Juliet said, reaching over my shoulder to grab a business card. "It's one of her special gifts. The Cho girls are always running at full throttle, Charlie. Anything less and we're letting the side down."

"We're a stereotype," Josie sighed.

I watched as Jade backed her way into the kitchen, carrying a tray of plates and glasses. She didn't look happy at all and I felt a pang of guilt at my overwhelming joy at being a normal kid for a night.

"Don't worry about it," Josie said. "We have thick skins. Take this back to the customer, no charge."

I took the receipt and change back to the customer at the door and then made my way through the restaurant towards the kitchen. Jade came out again with a red face, stopped three steps into the restaurant and turned back to the doors. I could see her fists clench and then she stormed back into the kitchen.

My danger sense was tingling.

I weaved my way through tables and made it to the kitchen doors, swinging them open, just as Jade whipped out a meat cleaver and swung it over her head. Momma Cho was leaning across the stainless steel bench, spectacles perched on the end of her nose.

She was shouting in Chinese, which, it may surprise you, I don't actually understand. My genius lies in the sciences. I can translate high end Maths and chemistry, but languages are all just clashing of sounds to me.

Jade fired back at her mother, shouting and slamming the cleaver down into a rump of pork. I could tell she was crying, and part of me felt like tearing up too.

"Hey, you guys," I said and stopped as they both looked at me.

"What you want?" Momma Cho asked and I felt like running away back up to the apartment behind the black lacquered door. "You see my daughter? Not a good girl."

"She's a great girl," I shot back. "Really, Mrs Cho, Jade is amazing."

Jade fumbled with her phone, jamming her thumb to

turn it off even as it beeped twice. Her eyes were puffy and red.

"No good," Momma Cho said.

"She's my best friend, and I haven't had one of them before, Mrs Cho. She's a good girl."

Momma Cho lay down the knife and folded her thick arms across her apron. She did not looked convinced.

"And Luca loves her, and we wouldn't even know half the things about this place if it wasn't for Jade."

"She talk too much on phone," Momma Cho said.

"We all do that," I said. "It's just what we do. We like to be connected."

"It's okay, Charlie, don't worry," Jade said.

"No, it does matter and I do worry. Jade's probably just feeling out of it because she was away today."

Momma Cho's eyebrows fused together, her eyes squinted hard.

"What?"

"Charlie…"

"Everyone was worried about her today, because she was sick," I said.

Jade held her head in her hands and sobbed. Three, hard sobs. I felt my stomach tighten. The kitchen wasn't so warm and friendly anymore.

"You no go to school?"

"Uh oh…" I said.

Chapter Twelve
Scoot

THE BAY SPREAD before me, all laid out in blues and shades of green where underwater rocks and seaweed lurked. The little beach below me was like a postcard: white sand and the constant ebb and flow of small crested waves. It wasn't a proper surf beach but it'd be fun to jump the waves like we used to as kids. And it was nothing like the industrious machine of the Melbourne ports. We'd spent some time hidden amongst the shipping containers and all the salt and the damp. This bay was a completely different world.

I looked along the foreshore to the south, my attention drawn by sounds of barbecue and family. A couple of kids were throwing a frisbee, their excitable terrier springing in all directions trying to run intercept. Further along some brightly coloured play equipment and beyond that was Will's promised land: the Henty Bay Skatepark.

I cupped my hand over my eyes to keep the sun out and tried to pick him out. There were a few skateboarders but they all looked the same from up on the bluff. I turned to Luca who was throwing sticks off the cliff, smirking as they pirouetted down to the little beach. I felt a premonition overcome me watching him there on the edge. The little kid would be the perfect candidate for a cliffside fatality.

"Dude, can you not stand so close to the edge?"

Luca dropped the last of his sticks and walked ahead of me towards the downward path. He wasn't talking to me since I'd forgotten to bring home food from Cho's kitchen. I tried to explain that Jade and her mum weren't really in a good mood, and that it was pretty much my fault, but Luca was still stuck on the fact I hadn't brought home his dinner.

"We'll get donuts later, okay?" I called to him, and he started running away from me faster. I wondered how many other families had days like this. I also wondered whether it would be unethical to buy a leash for my little brother.

When we finally arrived on flat ground the sun was really beating down on us. I pulled off my jacket and tied the sleeves around my waist, hoping not to look too unfashionable. The foreshore was fairly well populated with families and kids. It was actually pretty nice.

The skate park itself looked like what you'd expect if a train carrying concrete pipes had a nasty run-in with an industrial crane swinging a rainbow. It was a complete mess. Luca didn't seem to care, as usual, and started a run up the half-pipe. He scampered on his hands and knees, dodging the skaters and getting rust coloured stains on his new jeans. Dad would kill me.

If he wasn't half the size of a mouse. And if he wasn't missing.

"Luca, get off that," I called out, trying to ignore the death-stares I was getting from the boys and girls skating

past. The whirl of wheels and street clothes made me anxious. I didn't belong here. My whole life was now a flip-flop game of feeling good about Henty Bay and feeling absolutely crap.

"You're supposed to have wheels, kid," Will said right beside me. He was standing on a scooter, towering over me in a white tank top, shorts and a black beanie. I guess it was his casual setting.

"Cool!" Luca called and bounded over in five huge steps, hands grabbing for the scooter. "That's a different one."

Will let Luca pull the scooter away and stepped down next to me, hands automatically shoved into the pockets of his shorts.

"Yeah, man, my old ride's gone missing."

"Stolen?" I asked, feeling my face redden. I tried to remember where I'd tossed the miniaturised scooter. It was probably in a bird's nest by now.

Will shrugged.

"Dunno," he said. "But there's been a bit of a burglary blitz lately."

Luca shot off through the obstacle course at the park, careening up ramps and then around little poles. I lost interest quickly and went to sit at a bench. Will followed and sat down next to me.

"Um, thanks for that," I said, waving towards Luca. "He loves to get out every now and then."

"Yeah, I heard he did some cool stuff at the chemist. Hey, what's the deal with your dad?"

"Whattyamean?" I said quickly, dropping the physics

book I'd pulled out of my bag. It tumbled to the grass and Will leapt forward and grabbed it before I could react. He brushed off some loose grass and smiled at the title before handing it back to me.

"That's a heavy book," he said. "I thought we were here on a date."

"Yeah, well, Dad wanted me to… er, catch up on homework and stuff. He doesn't know it's a date, so… yeah, why're you interested?"

"In you?" he asked, blushing.

"I meant my dad."

"No reason," he lied. "Just haven't seen him around. Nakaya said some weird stuff yesterday and … anyhow, it's not really a date, right?"

"No way," I said.

A woman pushed a baby stroller past us, talking wildly into her phone while the baby grabbed upward to the brightly coloured giraffe toys dangling just out of reach. The woman's bare feet made me want to embrace summer. I looked over my shoulder towards the water's edge. It looked inviting.

"Hey, weird thing," Will said. "There's been a bunch of baby booster seats going missing."

"Are you deliberately using alliteration?" I asked.

"Maybe. But seriously, Dad said there've been ten reported thefts this week. And that's weird where we come from."

"Ten booster seats? From cars?"

"Yeah, but the cars aren't missing, just the seats. So,

that and all the gold thefts is making Dad a bit cranky. Started yelling at the TV last night. Like, right in the middle of Family Feud."

Gold. It was shiny and valuable. I felt a little bit sick as I sat next to Will who kept on chattering about his family. I wanted to listen, but my mind was racing through the probabilities of my Dad being involved in the recent string of thefts. Gold, definitely. Even before being shrunk by the Reducer, Dad was attracted to expensive, shiny objects. With his brain shrunk and his inhibitions obliterated, gold was totally beyond anything he could resist.

And the baby seats made me feel sad. Maybe Dad couldn't help himself when he saw the seats in cars. Somewhere inside his little, primitive brain, maybe he knew he had us to look after. Maybe, somehow he was trying to protect us.

It was a stretch, but unfortunately, it wasn't beyond the realm of possibility.

Dad was on a stealing spree.

"And that's how the whole lipstick thing happened," Will said and laughed. I smiled, obviously too late to understand the punch-line.

"You are a cool guy, Will," I said.

"Hey, I think maybe I better go and help your brother."

We both looked across the park and saw Luca talking with two other kids, roughly his own height. Beyond them, I saw five girls walking in a straight line towards the barbecue area which lay just in front of the skate park.

It was weird, but as the girls moved closer, families packed up and left. Kids moved to the water's edge and even the seagulls flew out of their way. Will stood up and jogged towards Luca, even as some of the other skaters decided it was time to go seek food for lunch. Wheels turned and the park emptied.

The girls stopped at the edge of the park and leaned against the wire fence, talking closely together and whipping up their phones to take shots of each other and some of the people around the area.

Will guided Luca back and pulled out his wallet, a wide (and exaggerated) smile plastered on his face.

"Let's get some chips," he said.

"Donuts," Luca said.

"Whatever. Let's go."

I stood up and lifted my bag to my shoulder, but I wasn't leaving just yet. Will refused to look back at the girls. One of them was stretching her arms up along the wire, her skimpy outfit stretching along with her body. There was a lot of skin there, even for such a hot day.

"Who are they?" I asked.

"Hmm?"

"Are they girls from school?"

Will handed off ten dollars to Luca who got a head start towards the strip of shops along the street. He scratched the back of his neck and nodded.

"Yeah, bad news."

"I don't see Nakaya there," I said.

"Nah, this isn't Nakaya's thing," he said, smiling. "This is pure evil."

"Funny, I've seen pure evil and that isn't it," I said.

"That girl kind of looks like Nakaya."

"I'm not going to look," Will said. "It's bad luck, and besides, it's probably Harriet. Nakaya's cousin."

"So the whole family's bad?"

"No," Will shot back quickly. "Nakaya's not like that."

"Facts suggest otherwise," I said, but I was getting tired of worrying about girls in this town. "They look pretty harmless to me."

"Let's just hope they don't get your phone number," Will said. "Come on, your brother's going to spend all my pocket money."

We walked slowly up the path. Our hands swung as we walked, almost touching, but not quite. They moved together though, and that was something.

"It is weird though, that someone's nicking booster seats," Will said.

"And gold," I added, trying to distance our conversation from any possible link to my father. Of course, gold was probably a terrible conversation subject. "Hey, I bet Miss Monzote is in trouble. She'd better watch out for the Gold Thief."

Will laughed and our hands touched for the briefest moment.

"She is pretty awesome," Will said. "I reckon she could handle herself."

"Yeah, there's that," I said. "Plus, it's probably fake."

"Nah."

"Yeah, totally fake."

Chapter Thirteen
Night Games

BEING PRETTY SURE that Dad was involved in the recent Henty Bay crime spree, I did what Mum always pressed for me to do: I took action. First, I completed my Maths homework (don't judge me), then I took Luca over to his friend's house for a sleepover, only it turned out that his new best friend was Taram Park, Nakaya's little brother. It also turned out that Luca and Taram have been exchanging tall tales of the family kind, so now I know why Nakaya said that stuff about my mum being in prison, and if I'm to believe Luca's story about Taram, the little Park kid actually invented Candy Crush.

I decided to have a 'Serious Talk' with Luca after I'd rescued Dad from himself, but I had to admit the little kid looked happy when I left him playing Skylanders with Taram. He looked like a normal eight year old. There was a definite pang in my stomach and I thought that Dad must have felt this way when he left us. He must have. And maybe that's why he was stealing baby booster seats from cars.

It sort of made sense to me.

With Luca safely in the hands of my enemy's family, I went to the library to try and use their computers to do a background check on Miss Monzote and her grisly, grey companion. We didn't have internet in the apartment, or even a computer and I felt prehistoric. The library was empty of kids, which didn't surprise me, given that it was Saturday, and apart from the three librarians who were chatting over cups of coffee and the New Release section I was on my own.

The local paper's website covered the local crime spree, so I quickly corroborated Will's story. Ten booster seats were stolen and there had been five break-ins involving the theft of gold. That was pretty major for a small town like Henty Bay. It hit the virtual front page of the paper, with two follow-up interview pieces.

Miss Monzote was a bit more interesting. She didn't have Facebook or Instagram or any other social media presence, which shouted out 'weird' to me, but it might just have been because she was old. Forty-two last March according to one of her teacher-friend's Facebook page. There were some odd photos of teachers celebrating her party at the museum. A wider search showed that she was pretty well educated, with degrees in anthropology and history spanning Europe, North America and South America. She'd moved a lot, following post graduate pathways that had popped up one after the other. How she became a history teacher at Henty Bay High School was a bit of a mystery. The latest hit I got on Miss Monzote was from a gala opening in Melbourne a year ago where she had been a speaker on 'The Maternal Mystique In Aztec Mythology' which seemed a bit forced to me.

Her grey bearded companion was a blank though. I had no name and no idea of what he had to do with anything. It was just so strange to see someone so cultured like Miss Monzote hanging with a scruffy old man, but maybe he was an academic. They seemed to come in all shapes and sizes; and smells. I closed my eyes at the terminal and tried to think away the odd dog smell I'd gotten from the man. It was kind of gross.

I left the library with a book so it didn't look like I'd just popped in to use their bandwidth, but I tossed it on the kitchen table when I got back into the apartment. Maybe, if things turned out well enough, and Dad was back to a normal, kind of useful size, then maybe I'd get a chance for recreational reading. The last piece of fiction I'd read was a book for school called Lockie Leonard, Human Torpedo. I kind of wished I had a human torpedo, of the military kind, right now. Shaking up the town to find my dad might have been a more successful plan than what I had. My plan was simply to go out and look around after dark. Fingers crossed, Dad would stumble by.

I pulled on my leather jacket and holstered the Medusa-Reducer, which was now fully functional, thanks to final tinkering after shrinking Will's scooter. It had enough battery charge to last a half dozen shots easily, and the solar energy extractor cells would kick in over the next few days for an almost limitless supply of energy.

I retrieved the last piece of equipment from my room. They were night binoculars with a bit of mad science thrown in. My Mum made them when I was eight, I think. Just before she went away. They were pretty cool, but kind of clunky. Maybe that made them even cooler.

As I walked down the stairs to the front door I wondered about Jade. I hadn't seen her since she'd had the blow up with her mum in the kitchen, and I was sure everyone knew it was my fault. My comment had sparked the fuse. Maybe I was a human torpedo after all. The Cho's restaurant was open but I kept my head down as I passed in front, hoping Mrs Cho wasn't about to burst out and grill me about Jade's absences, or worse still: hoping Jade wasn't going to chase me down the street with a meat cleaver.

Keeping to myself, which wasn't hard, I did a perimeter walk of the town centre. Most of the shops were closed, but a few were open and there were apparently enough people on the streets to keep gold thieves at bay. I circled the town again, and then did a street by street grid-walk which was just as thrilling as it sounds.

Eventually I stopped in front of the bright yellow comic shop, Culture Kit. The window was dominated by a four by four cube display, each with a bright four-colour comic in the centre. I stood with my hands in my jacket, looking half at the comic covers and half at my reflection.

The Celestial Knights had a new #1 out, apparently. Parhelion, Castus, Cyclone and some new woman with a shadowy cloak graced the cover. They were all over-sized biceps and shining teeth. Parhelion was a scientist in real life. I'd read up on him for a project in primary school. He was born in Botswana and worked his butt off to get into university. That's the bit I loved. It didn't matter that later he invented a 'parhelion' suit that allowed him to fly and all that superhero stuff. He cared about education, and I guess I saw that in me too.

Yes, I'm a nerd.

The door to the comic shop opened and a man walked out, holding the door open with his left foot as he struggled with keys and a cash box.

He saw me and smiled.

"We're closing up," he said. "Do you need anything now, before I turn the key?"

He dropped the cash box. I stooped down and picked it up, giving it a shake before handing it back to him.

"I think I need a hero," I said, turning back to the window display. "These Knights comics keep re-booting to #1."

"Yeah, marketing."

"But it's all the same thing," I said. "Every time they start again they have the same opening. Big bad guy threatens the world and the Knights are called together to save it."

The man nodded and locked the door.

"Yeah, it's a formula, but it works. Who doesn't like to imagine themselves as a superhero, coming in to save the day?"

I bit my bottom lip, thinking about all the talks I'd overheard between my dad and his minion mates. They had high dreams too, but none of them included saving the world, exactly.

"Have you tried something else?" the man asked, looking a lot less stressed now that he wasn't juggling his daily takings and trying to lock up. "There's more to comics than superheroes."

"You mean the indy stuff?" I asked.

He laughed.

"You are cynical, kid. Are you on holidays?"

"Nah, this is my home now," I said. "My family just moved here from the city."

"Well, come and look around when you get the chance. You might surprise yourself with these superhero comics. Great opportunity to escape whatever it is you're running from."

"I'm not running."

"No, you're staring into the window of a comic book store, going nowhere."

"You're a great salesman."

"I'm Jason."

"Charlie."

"Well, I'll expect to see you next week. We've got a shipment on Wednesday. Might even be a new Tales of Azambia #1 in there, and Nordkapp Man."

I couldn't help smiling at his enthusiasm, so I gave him a quick thumbs up and kept walking. It's weird how things turn out. Doctor Katlego Tsholofelo leaves Botswana, gets educated at King's College, invents a bunch of stuff and ends up as a real-life superhero, with his own ongoing monthly comic book. My dad drops out of school in Sunshine at fourteen, gets drafted into a Greek mafia gang when he's clearly Italian, and then goes on to become a professional minion for bigger, badder villains. Even got a name: The Undertaker. Classy.

But it's where he met my mum, and I guess if he hadn't have gone down that path I wouldn't be here at all. I just wish my mum could have had the chance to be great like Parhelion. She would have been happier.

Probably.

I end up at the foreshore, walking around the abandoned barbecues and seagulls cozying up for the night. It's so quiet but I can hear the ocean again: waves rolling up the sand, the suck and thwoosh of the water. I sit down as the sun slips away and pull my jacket tighter. I can feel the Medusa-Reducer and I check the clasp of the holster without looking. It's a nice view, looking out across the water. It's peaceful, but it's also lonely. I wish the whole family was here, sitting on the grass and getting a little chill as night comes along. And we could just sit there. There wouldn't be any fighting, no arguments, no cutting comments. Just some hot chips and a growing crowd of hungry white and grey sea birds.

When you hear sirens, there's usually three things you can do. Number one, you can ignore them and go on with your bystander life. Good luck with that. Number two, you can run away as fast as you can. I've had some experience with that. Number three, is you can run towards the sirens. Considering that I was looking for my dad and he was probably mixed up in criminal activities, I took the screech of sirens as a sign and followed the number three action.

The thing is, though, running up hills is not a good idea when you're lugging a hi-tech pistol and a clunky set of binoculars. In fact, in my opinion, running is totally over-rated in any situation. I grabbed the edge of the little wooden fence that topped the grassy hill and hauled myself over it, falling to my knees on the other side, heaving for breath.

I needed to go for morning runs again.

Or invent a flying machine.

The sirens were still ringing through the streets and I saw a few people start to come out of shops and houses, moving towards the noise, their fingers playing across smart phones as they kept everyone else up to date with what was happening.

There were three police cars outside the museum when I got there. I saw Josie and Juliet Cho out the front of the restaurant, but there was no sign of Jade. Uniformed policemen stood outside the double doors of the museum and kept everyone back. I spotted one of the journalists from the paper taking photos with his phone. While everyone was looking at the front entrance I looked around the street. It was such a bad move to hit the museum - even my Dad, with his half a miniature brain wouldn't be crazy enough to break into the front of a museum on the main street.

I was missing something.

Actually, everyone was missing something. The police were concentrated in one place. If there was a bad guy in all this, then they would be someplace else. It was clearly a distraction. I gave the Cho girls one last look in case their sister was there, but then double-backed to the next block. It was dark now, and while everyone was focusing on the lights and sounds of the main street, I decided to get some perspective; some elevated perspective.

I climbed up on to a rubbish bin next to a milk bar which was closed and then hoisted myself on to the veranda, scrambling to get a foot purchase before finally getting on to the roof. There was no way I could do that with an audience, but a success is a success in my book. I walked carefully up the slight incline of the veranda and then stepped up to the next shop's roof. I could see the beach again and a clear path for me to cross the buildings, looking for whatever had caused the false alarm at the museum.

At least, I hoped it was a false alarm.

After a few roof movements I got to the edge of the main street and crouched down, lowering myself to the rusted tin roof of what was probably the bakery. I pulled out the binoculars and adjusted the settings, bringing up infra red and the regular night-sight settings. The glare from the flashing lights faded quickly as I made some other adjustments.

The binoculars gave me a good view of the museum. There was no one inside any of the upper levels, and with the heat-sensor setting on, I counted five policemen inside on the ground floor. Power seemed to be off in the whole building, although the places either side were fine. A localised electrical burn-out seemed awfully convenient.

I swung the binoculars around and looked up and

down the street, searching for power fluctuations or heat signatures in the wrong place. Master Frank was obviously doing something requiring a lot of electricity at the back of the dojo, and with a few more adjustments I could make out a whole bunch of computers hooked up in the back of his place. He might have been a serious gamer or a pirate or any number of other things. But I didn't have time for him. I needed to find my dad.

And that's when I saw the kid on the bike again, shooting along a side street.

Dan.

I moved to follow him, carefully treading over the rooftops and avoiding the really tall ones, tracking his movement from above. He didn't go far, just two streets over, and I sat hunched against a chimney as he pulled off his helmet and threw it to the ground. The boy was pissed off.

He'd stopped outside a house and the garage door was open. A white van with the word 'Isagrim Removalists' stencilled across the side had its engine running and the back doors swung open. Two men were hoisting up children's booster seats. I was stuck on the roof of a house and at least a jump, combat roll and leap away from them. There was a set of council recycling bins next to a small sedan parked in the driveway and for a moment I thought about throwing myself at them, hoping to get to street level, but I'd only end up embarrassed and broken.

Dan went up to one of the men as I pondered my entry, and pushed him hard in the chest, knocking him back a few steps. The man was a rough kind of skinny. He dropped the seat and swung at Dan, but my 'go-to' man ducked easily and stepped out of reach.

"What are you doing?" he yelled at the pencil-thin man. I was wondering that myself. I pulled out the Medusa-Reducer, but before I could unleash it on the bean bag I'd spotted next to the recycling bins, Dan picked up the booster seat and tossed it into the back of the van. "You're supposed to wait for her, you idiots."

I didn't like the look of things down there. And then a shorter man ambled into view from the other side of the van and I liked it even less. It was the grey bearded man from the Cho's restaurant.

"You funny kid," the man said to Dan, edging his way closer, moving in a kind of circle. "I am running this operation."

I could see Dan's chest heaving like he was out of breath. He looked suddenly confused and ran his hands back through his hair. I noticed he was geared up in some kind of motorcross outfit, with padded gloves and trousers and thick-soled boots. He looked bad-ass.

"We're family, so I will be kind," the man said, coming close to Dan, and then, in a flash, he punched Dan in the stomach hard. Dan doubled over and hit the road with his gloved hands wrapped around his stomach, his body heaving with the effort of trying to breathe. The bearded man kicked him in the ribs and Dan collapsed.

I stood up and raised the Medusa-Reducer again, firing off a shot at the sad looking bean bag. I had it on reverse. A blast of white energy whipped outward and struck the bag, and it started to shudder, rippling, twisting in the night. And then it grew.

The bearded man and his two cronies were surprised, but since I'd built the thing and knew what it did, I was only quietly impressed and wasted no time. I leapt off the roof even as the bag was still growing and hit it with a soft, welcome sound. I rolled down its side and landed impressively at the end of the drive. I'd had enough training in judo to successfully pull off a rooftop jump into a giant beanbag.

"Let's even the odds here," I said, switching the settings and firing my gun. I hit one of the cronies with the paralysing beam, and even though I had been aiming for the bearded man, it wasn't a surprise that I missed. There's an unwritten rule about leaving the big bad guy till last.

"Who is this?" the man asked, as if on cue. I think he looked impressed.

"The police are on their way," I lied. "You can stop loading those booster seats and tell me where the little guy is."

I expected Dad to leap to the man's shoulder and start laughing at me, like it was all a big joke. At the very least, I expected the bearded man to take me seriously. Instead, he laughed. He slapped his knees with his hands and had a great belly laugh. On the ground in front of him, Dan pulled himself together enough to turn his head in my direction.

"Where is he?" I shouted again.

"I am the big man," the bearded man said, straightening

himself up. "There is no little man."

"But the burglaries…"

I hadn't seen where the second crony went, which was an amateur mistake, so when he grabbed at me from behind I think I probably deserved to go down hard. He had his arms around me quickly and with his momentum and my awkward footing, we both went down. I dropped the Medusa-Reducer but I used the fall to shift my weight so the crony took the brunt of the impact. I twisted my legs around his and bent his knee back which was enough of a surprise to immobilise him while I jabbed him in the ribs with my elbow.

"This is so funny, Danny Boy!" cried the bearded man. "I love this town."

I crawled away from the man, kicking him in the hand as he grabbed for me. I could see into the van from the low angle and I saw gold: watches and chains and so on. This was the right operation. I grabbed the Medusa-Reducer and stood up again, swinging it around to aim at the man on the ground. I didn't hesitate and zapped him with the paralyser. It came apart in my hands, but it worked. All the hard work I'd put into fixing the thing and now it was falling apart again.

"Nice toy," the bearded man said. "I can appreciate such a thing, but surely it is not your own."

Dan stood up with the assistance of the van. He looked a wreck, but it was clear he recognised me. It's funny that I've never even thought about using a mask. You'd think I would have learned from my father, but then again, he's had his fair share of masks and funny outfits, and he's still been busted more times than we've had hot roasts on Sunday.

"I must know," the man said. "Who are you?"

"The end of the line," I said.

"Dan, take care of her and meet us at midnight."

With that line, the man turned and ran. I wasn't expecting him to run, or to run so fast, but the old man had a nice pair of legs on him. For a split second I didn't know what to do. Dan was winded and bruised, two other criminals were frozen in the street and there was a van full of evidence.

"Don't move," I said to Dan and then ran after the old man.

The streets were dark. None of the street lights were working, and the houses also looked like the power was down. I know it's still no surprise that I hate running, but taking off down a darkened street after a man who steals baby booster seats and beats up on kids was probably one of the biggest mistakes of my life here in Henty Bay.

As I passed a parked car, a burst of light exploded all around me. Flares shot up from the ground, stunning me and making everything turn upside down. I reached out to steady myself but all I got was open air. I hit the road again, for the second time that night.

I squeezed my eyes shut but all I saw were more dancing lights.

I could tell he was out there, just out of reach. I could hear heavy breathing. I think I could even smell him, that wet dog smell I'd caught at the restaurant.

"So perhaps you can answer me now," his voice called out. "Or do I have to kick it out of you, Fraulein? Who are you? Who do you work for?"

I could have told him. I could have terrified the little man with the truth.

But my eyes cleared. The lights were still having a party at the edges of my vision but the middle bits were clear enough. He was leaning down, hands on his knees, eyes squinting at me like he really was trying to figure out what a fourteen year old girl was doing running around the night with a ray gun.

"I do have ways to make you talk," he said, standing up again and slipping his hand into his jacket pocket. He brought it out again and there was a silver ball bearing. He began rolling between his two fingers. I had a feeling it wasn't an ordinary piece of metal.

"Bite me," I said. I had the Reducer in my hand, and fired it at the ground beneath his feet. The road pulled in on itself, its surface cracked and then disappeared altogether leaving the man unbalanced. He stumbled and dropped the ball. I shook my head again to clear my vision and then picked up the second part of my weapon. I reversed the settings and fired at the ground again, enlarging it to engulf his shoes.

The man yelped, but he was stuck.

"Maybe you've got some answers," I said, still keeping my distance. The man was pulling hard at his feet. I scooped up the little ball bearing and pocketed it. "Who is behind all this?"

"You shall regret this, little demon. You shall very much regret this."

"Is my Dad a part of this?"

I was losing it. I knew it.

There was a screech of tyres and more bright lights swung around to smack me in the face, only this time it was the headlights of a car.

Busted.

There was a yowl from the old man and even though I couldn't see him I knew he'd yanked his feet free. Car doors opened and slammed shut again. I stood in the street, hand shielding my eyes. I saw a silhouette near the car door but it didn't move, just looked at me stuck in the headlights.

And then they left. More car doors slamming and the screech of a getaway.

I heard the sounds of people coming out of their houses, but I couldn't leave without checking where I'd ripped up the road. Apart from some funky grey-brown hair left behind there was nothing left of the bearded man. I didn't have time for a full forensic sweep so I ran towards a house and crashed my way through some bushes into their backyard. Luckily there was no dog, so I high tailed it over their back fence and out of the area, leaving the residents to start making up explanations.

After doubling back to the museum, where I saw Sergeant Chase looking lost and confused, I found my way to the cliffs. I felt like everything was just out of reach and I needed to know that Luca was okay. The Parks lived in a nice street overlooking the bay. On one side of the road were orange brick houses with a definite beach holiday feel to them, and on the other side was lush green lawns and then the cliffs and then the water. I walked with the ocean still in my ears and despite not finding Dad, I was coming to a kind of peace about things. Things might still have been bad, but at least Dad wasn't involved.

When I saw Dan's bike leaning up against the low brick fence of the Parks' house I nearly lost it again. He was working for the grey bearded man. He was a low life criminal. I saw movement in the front window of the house. I shook my head in disbelief. Not only was he a criminal, he was actually a burglar and he was inside Nakaya's house, probably stealing booster seats.

I was only going to walk past the house and check to see if Luca was okay, but seeing someone lurking behind the curtains of the front room I figured I might as well get some well-earned payback on Dan Galkin. I stepped over the low fence and tip-toed across the manicured lawn, pulling up my bincoulars to read heat signatures.

There was a figure walking around, that was certain, but there was a second one lying down in a horizontal, sleeping position. It was a burglary.

Back in the city I'd probably punch my way through the window, but this wasn't Melbourne. It was my home, and I didn't want to go around wrecking other people's things, even if it did belong to Nakaya's family. I crept to the window instead and examined it from the outside.

It wasn't locked.

It didn't even have a lock.

"That is a serious lapse in security, Mr and Mrs Park," I mumbled to myself. Using the binoculars I tracked what had to be Dan and then slowly pushed the window up when he was busy at the other end of the room. The window slid up easily and without a sound. Trust the Parks to clean their windows and keep them well-oiled.

It didn't take much to pull myself in through the window, but I did slither a bit too much as I moved and ended up only half nailing the landing. I pulled myself together and took in the room.

Dan stood by a dressing table. It was definitely him. There was a faint light coming from his hand and it lit up his face as he turned around. His shaved blonde hair with the lightning bolt symbol and his piercing dark eyes were unmistakable.

I saw his hand glowing. It wasn't a torch or even a phone. It was his hand. Blue light came from under his skin, little rivers of blue energy which looked like veins. And in his other hand was a bunch of gold stuff: chains and jewellery bags and a military medal with a red, white and blue sash.

"Will you stop stalking me?" he hissed. There was a backpack on the floor next to his boots and he dropped the stolen goods into its open jaws. "The old man might wake up, so keep your lecture to yourself."

I looked over to the man in the bed. He was lying on his back and had his mouth open. He had dark skin and the lines on his face made him look really, really tired, even when he was asleep. It was a single bed. The whole room looked kind of bare, apart from the dressing table which had a bunch of feminine things on it, like hair brushes and adjustable mirrors and photo frames. It was all old though.

"You can't seriously be stealing this stuff," I hissed, stepping closer.

"Okay," Dan agreed. "I'm not."

He picked up the bag and slung it over his shoulder. As he stepped past me I grabbed the bag and tugged hard, spinning him back around to face me. His glowing hand pulsed brighter and we both noticed it. I noticed it, and he noticed me notice it.

"I don't want to talk about it," he said, still harsh but quiet.

I pulled the bag again and he lost his grip on it.

"That stays here," I said. "I thought I could trust you."

"You did not."

"Yes, I did, actually. You know what I did, what I took from the school, but I didn't hurt anyone."

Dan narrowed his eyes, darkly.

"I'm not hurting anyone either, genius. I'm just taking some stuff that I need. There's no difference between us."

I put my hand against his chest to stop him moving towards the bag. He was probably right about the morality of both our actions, but I wasn't going to let him walk out with some old guy's stuff.

"I needed that stuff to save my dad," I said.

Dan smiled but it wasn't a friendly smile. It looked kind of dead, actually. Like he was lost.

"And I need this stuff to save my Dad," he said.

He grabbed my wrists which were holding him back

and both his hands surged. I felt a burn and then I was thrown backward and into the wall like I'd been shocked. As soon as I landed I scrambled for the bag. Dan was on the ground grabbing for it too, but I pulled it away quicker and then fell back into the dresser, smashing things to the ground.

I heard noises outside the door and the old man turned in his sleep.

"Give me the bag," Dan said, louder. "Give it to me!" he shouted. His eyes flashed with blue energy and I could feel my hair standing on end as the whole room started to crackle with electricity. The bedside clock radio flashed, numbers flicking around backwards and forwards. The radio turned on to loud static. The bedroom light flashed on and then exploded.

Dan was losing it.

"No," I said. "You're not a thief."

The door crashed open and Nakaya and Mrs Park burst in. The old man sat up in his pyjamas, clutching at his chest, his mouth moving in silence like he was swallowing the air around him.

I lunged out at Dan but missed him. He turned to the window and jumped out, setting the curtains on fire as he moved through them. I scrambled after him but he was already over the fence and on his bike.

"What the hell?" Nakaya shouted. "Conti?"

I turned back to Nakaya and her mother, who was comforting the man in the bed. I held out the backpack to her and then pulled at the curtains, ripping them off the runners and stomping on them to put out the fires.

"I think you guys might need to install some locks on your windows," I said.

Nakaya Park brought over a cup of hot chocolate to where I was sitting at her family's kitchen breakfast bar. She'd put in two pink marshmallows which kind of reminded me of the fluffy pink dressing gown she was wearing.

The police had come and gone. I'd given statements to Will's dad, which was awkward, but he seemed satisfied that I'd just been curious after all the hooplah at the museum earlier that night. I didn't tell him about Dan, but gave a physical description of a kid I knew back in the city. I tried not to embellish it too much.

Luca and Taram hadn't even woken up.

Mrs Park had gone back to her husband's room at the front and was going to sit with him through the night. Nakaya was keen to get rid of me, but she couldn't refuse me a hot chocolate for my heroism. That had been Mr Chase's idea. As he left, he'd called me a hero.

How little did he know?

"So that was my dad," Nakaya said, sliding the mug across the laminex to my waiting hands.

"Uh-huh."

I didn't want to make a comment. There was no way I'd have pictured him as Nakaya's father. Sure, the mum was a perfect fit. Super-tanned skin, bleached hair and an attitude that I'd come up against at Master Frank's dojo. Like mother, like daughter.

"He has Alzheimer's," Nakaya said. "Early onset."

I nodded.

"He was a lawyer, you know? Worked here in Henty Bay for twenty years. He was a great man."

"You keep saying 'was'," I said softly.

Nakaya shrugged and I could see tears in her eyes. I didn't even know she had tear ducts.

"He hardly remembers anything," she said. "But those bloody war medals are his Dad's and he remembers them. It's the only thing that keeps him here, you know? It's his anchor, and you … you kind of saved them for us. Saved him, probably. God knows what would happen if he lost them."

I reached across and patted her hand, which was immediately awkward. I didn't know what to do so I sort of kept my hand there, close by. She looked at it and then at me and sniffed.

"I owe you one, Conti," she said softly.

"Okay," I said.

"One. Understand? One."

I nodded and stood up, leaving the two little marshmallows to rock against each other in the mug, slowly melting into sticky oblivion.

"You know, my Dad's gone, right?" I said. "I don't know where he is."

"When?"

"I don't know. A couple of days."

Nakaya frowned.

"I'm sorry," she said. "Oh my God, are you crying?"

I reached my fingers up to my cheeks and realised I was. I was bloody crying. And Nakaya started crying too. Somehow I ended up hugging her and as I smelled her super-clean hair and felt her overly-fluffy dressing gown, I realised that no one was who they appeared to be. No one was as evil as you'd think, and no one was as perfect or happy or sad or intelligent or popular as you want to paint them.

We've all got problems, I thought - almost shouted out loud, really.

Jade was probably trembling over text messages, crying herself into the night. Dan was probably getting pushed around by his family. Nakaya was desperately holding on to a false image. And I was trying to be the perfect daughter while my Dad was out somewhere not giving a damn about us at all.

I never did finish the hot chocolate but Nakaya threw some pillows at me and gave me a spare doona so I could sleep on the couch in the super-sized lounge room. I tried to shrug it off and go home, but there was nothing for me back there. I was alone and I felt so cold.

Chapter Fourteen
A Not-Completely-Terrible Monday

O N MONDAY EVERYONE turned up to school pretending our lives were good and the world was fine and dandy. After Will and I escorted Luca to his school, complete with some impressive scooter tricks, we caught up with our class which huddled together outside the school gates. We were going to the museum to look at really old dead people and ancient pottery that no one was interested in.

Jade turned up late, but I grabbed her immediately and told her I'd never, ever again betray our friendship like I had. Will also promised never to betray either of us, and with his puppy-dog eyes and a hug from me, Jade started laughing. She had been grounded, that was true, but it wasn't so bad. Extra work, no TV and her phone was confiscated.

I figured that was a blessing in disguise.

"Come along children," Miss Monzote called. She was wearing a close-fitting black dress and strappy sandals that curled up to her knees. "Today you will be indulging me and learning amazing stories about life thousands of years ago.

If you are not suitably impressed by nightfall, then I shall positively flay myself alive for failing you all."

There was a bit of laughter, but I couldn't help imagining her whipping herself to death. Considering her bearded friend had probably tried to kill me over the weekend, I wasn't about to give her the benefit of the doubt. I knew she was involved in whatever was happening in Henty Bay.

"Hey, you think there'll be chocolate?" Will asked as we started moving along the street, heading to the city centre.

"Why?" Jade asked.

"I'm thinking about becoming, you know, vegetarian."

I smiled but walked on without commenting. When we arrived in the main street the whole class stopped and watched a battle unfold in the middle of the road.

A man was dressed as Southern Cross, his blue and white suit extremely tight and revealing. A second man was wearing a replica Parhelion costume. The dark blue cape flew behind him and he pointed across at a second costumed man who was wearing one of those commercial costumes you can get of The Witch Doctor. It came with in-built muscle suit but the mask looked very flimsy.

I couldn't hear what they were saying, but Will nudged me as we stood there waiting for the theatrics to pass.

"They do this every month," Will said. He pointed across at the comic shop. "That's Simon and Jason. I think Simon's the guy in the Southern Cross suit."

"You know Southern Cross doesn't wear a cape, right?" I asked.

"Details," Will said. "The other guy's John and he owns

Primo's Comics, over there."

I followed Will's out-stretched arm and saw a second comic shop, plastered with posters. I'd never seen it before, and it was tightly squeezed in between a bank and a laundromat.

"Why are there two comic shops?" I asked.

"What do you mean?"

I gestured to the men and then to their shops.

"Why are there two shops in one little town?"

The men started to fight. The Witch Doctor swung his rather impressive looking replica staff and connected with what looked like a lightsaber. Parhelion, who was most likely Jason - the guy I'd met the other night when he was closing the shop - swung the lightsabre thing low and made the Witch Doctor jump. The crowd cheered. The staff swung back at Jason but he countered again with his lightsaber. There was a clashing sound and the Southern Cross guy threw water bombs. A few kids laughed. Even Miss Monzote seemed to be enjoying the battle.

"Are they allowed to do this? Like, in the middle of the street?" I asked.

"Yeah, sure," Will said. "It's not against the law or anything."

I thought that maybe reconstructing an epic battle in the middle of a street was possibly a crime, but Will would know better than me. We waited patiently for another five minutes and then the battle ended. The Witch Doctor took off his feathered war-mask and shouted out to the crowd that there'd be 20% off everything. The Southern Cross guy offered a free comic to all customers, and then the men hugged each other and we all just sort of walked on, as if nothing had happened.

"So last night…" Will said. "I heard that you broke into Nakaya's house."

"No," I said, shooting a look to Miss Monzote who was standing like a shepherd at the entrance to the museum. "I slept on her couch."

"Told you she wasn't that bad."

"You slept on her couch?" Jade asked. "Why?"

"Dad's gone."

"What?" Will said. Jade grabbed my hand and squeezed it.

"No big deal," I said. "Guys, it's fine."

Miss Monzote tapped me lightly on the head as we passed into the museum, counting the students.

"Lucky thirteen," she said.

I smiled at her quickly but let it drop as soon as I was inside. Jade pulled at my hand.

"Where is he?" she asked.

"I don't know. Maybe the city?" I said, with the rise of a question tagged on the end. I hoped she would let it drop.

There was a chime from Jade's bag and all three of us looked at it like it was a bomb.

"Is that a phone?" Will asked. "I thought your mum took it away."

Jade quickly pulled it out and turned away, reading the text. I reached around and slipped it out of her hand. Jade grabbed for it but I batted away her attempts.

"This is horrible," I said.

"It's nothing," Jade said. "Just a stupid…"

"No, seriously, this is hurtful. She's telling you to die, like, right to your face."

"She doesn't mean it."

"It's right here," Charlie said. "And there's these other texts. You have to take this to the police."

"No," Jade grabbed the phone back. "Just leave it alone, okay?"

Miss Monzote appeared behind us and lay her hands on Will's shoulders, giving them a quick squeeze. Jade shoved the phone back into her bag.

"Let us begin our amazing journey," Miss Monzote purred.

"Oh it's begun," I mumbled. I looked at the creepy poster of an Aztec goddess. It looked like she was going to leap out and eat us. There were crazy eyes and too-sharp teeth.

Miss Monzote explained the exhibition; the focus on women's lives and the religions. Some of the kids openly yawned but she didn't acknowledge them. She talked about the goddess on the poster - Chalchiuhtlicue. She was a goddess of children and pregnancy and water and even tortoises. Miss Monzote clutched the amulet around her neck and started telling us all about her life in the Andes and then up through Mexico. It probably was interesting but all I heard from her lips was sound. I wasn't listening. I was watching.

We drifted through exhibits including some ordinary-looking pottery. You'd have thought that ancient stuff would look impressive, but it's all just clay in the end. I did stop at one table, though, when I saw the flat looking vase I'd seen at the Cho's Restaurant. I leaned closer and read the signage. It was a sacrificial dish. No surprise there. The lid was used to secure essence: the trapped life of victims.

I imagined how Jade was feeling, getting those hurtful texts all the time. I wondered how much essence she had left. I would have to do something about that. I could feel a kind of growing fire in my belly: a fire of retribution. Maybe the Aztecs were influencing me, or maybe I was sick of the world spiralling out of my control?

I straightened up and looked across at Miss Monzote who was fawning over the poster of Chalchiuhtlicue, pointing out the markings on the goddess's body and making the kids smile. It was the end of the tour.

We spent more time in the gift shop than in the exhibit. Kids bought postcards and keychains and other worthless junk. I kept my hands in the pockets of my jeans.

Outside, Will slipped his hand into my pocket and pulled out my hand. I was amazed at the warmth of his hand, his fingers entwined in mine. It was a sudden jolt of strangeness. I was caught off guard.

"I got you this," he said, looking down at me while we stood so close. He pressed a snow globe into my hands and smiled. "You shake it up and snow falls on the museum."

I nodded and he let go of my hands. I looked down at the globe and instead of seeing some piece of tourist junk, I think I saw magic. I gave it a shake and walked on next to Will and Jade.

"So what do you think?" he asked.

"Yeah, it's pretty cool."

"Reckon I could hold your hand on the way back?"

"I reckon you could, Mister Chase," I said.

Chapter Fifteen
Gather the War Party

BACK AT SCHOOL I soon realised Dan Galkin was a no-show. At the end of recess I cornered Will at his locker, holding his locker door closed as he tried to get his books.

"Do you know where Dan is?"

"No," Will said, smiling with his dopey eyes all bright and adorable. We'd been holding hands on the way back but once we hit the school I didn't know what to do, so we just sort of left in different directions. I'd ended up sitting with Jade in the courtyard and neither of us wanted to talk about our problems.

"But I need to see him," I said. Today was going to be about settling scores. I had the Reducer part of the Medusa-Reducer in my pocket, ready for another test run. I'd spent hours fixing it so it wouldn't come loose again like it did when wrestling with the bearded man. "It's kind of urgent."

"He misses a lot of school, Charlie," Will said. "Kind of messed up."

"Do you have his phone number?"

"I don't think he even has a phone, or none that I've seen."

"He's gotta have a phone. He's a teenager."

Will shrugged.

"Why are you so interested? He's not even in our year."

"He said he'd get me some stuff and I kind of want to give him some stuff too. Nothing exciting, Will, just something he's got coming to him.

"Well, his family is really messed up."

"You said that."

"I know, but you reckon you got the weird card? His mum's, like, blue. Like, really blue."

"Yeah, right," I let him open his locker and looked up and down the corridor. Dan was out of reach, but I smiled when I saw a familiar group of girls walking towards me, Nakaya's cousin front and centre. "I'll catch you later, okay? I've got to do some stuff at lunch time."

"Stuff? What stuff?" Will asked. I saw the sadness in his eyes as I ripped away another opportunity to hang out together.

"Just girl stuff."

"Oh," he said, stepping back, eyes wide. "Okay."

The pack of girls rolled out of the Student Services office and spread like a fog - a poisonous fog. Other kids gave them a wide berth, never making eye contact but maybe dropping a few hollow insults or jokes before rushing into the canteen.

I'd seen them hassle kids before. They searched for weakness, acquired a target and descended. It was crazy. These girls were so desperate not to get hurt, not to be the isolated one, that a kind of bloodlust came over them. Harriet was the worst. She never led the attacks but she was always there, pulling the proverbial strings and pushing all the right buttons.

And Harriet was Nakaya's cousin. I looked across at my temporary ally, hearing her words from the night before: 'The enemy of my enemy is my friend.' We both knew they were just words, and actually, looking at my family history that doesn't really ring true in any way whatsoever. But the words were enough for us to put away the hatchets for a day so we could sort out Harriet Gould.

Nakaya didn't look especially impressed with the girls who were already shoving a Year 7 girl who had somehow found herself cut off from everyone else. Nakaya didn't look impressed at anything, really, and certainly not with the idea of being in my company.

"Let's do it," she said, flexing her fingers and cracking her knuckles.

"Oh my God, you're like Kung-Fu Barbie," I said, smiling at her sudden scowl.

"And you're like that sad little fish that no one has the heart to bash on the head, so it just sits there flapping around like a joke."

"Yeah, you might want to work on your insults," I said.

"It wasn't an insult," Nakaya said. "I was being nice."

"Hilarious. Come on, let's fix these whirling

demonspawn," I said. "At least we can agree on that."

Harriet and the mob had nearly broken Jade and I couldn't let them keep up the carnage. Already they had the little blonde girl in tears. They moved close to her, calling out insults, then retreated so another could take her place.

I'd only been at the school for a couple of weeks, but these girls were wreaking more chaos than Captain Calamari and his pirates had during the whole Port Melbourne Intifada last year. And that had made all the papers and the TV news. No one seemed to be overly concerned about what Harriet was up to.

I'd found Jade crying in the toilets during third period. She wouldn't let me see her phone, but the message was clear: I had to do something.

"Let's roll," Nakaya said, and pulled herself up and over the fence, landing like a celebrity cat, ready for an intervention.

The plan was easy. I'd organised more complicated stings in kindergarten, but given the rising weirdness around the museum and Miss Monzote I didn't have time for premium level payback. Harriet and the other predators would have to settle for some budget Conti justice.

Nakaya and I walked to the edge of the school driveway, stopping spitting distance from the other girls. Don't judge me: it's a serious description of distance and practical for school kids. Harriet shifted her place, letting two of the bigger girls take the front, but I could see her wide grin and devious eyes. I imagined her behind her computer screen, firing off one liners or with her thumbs pressing out hateful texts.

"So, I'll accept your apology," I said flatly.

"Don't confuse them," Nakaya said. "They don't get sarcasm."

"What are you two lesbians on about?" a tall girl asked, followed by uniform sneers from the front row.

"Just wanted to give you a chance to end this before you burst into tears," I said. Most of them already had their phones out. I could tell I'd been photographed already and one of them was filming.

"You can't bully us, Nakaya Park," the tall girl said. "We have rights."

I looked across at Nakaya, wondering how this had become a thing about us bullying them, and then I realised I hadn't exactly spelled it out to them. I was still angry about the text messages and the way Jade had crumpled every time she got them.

"Shut up," I said, stepping forward into their space. "Your squad of banshees are terrorising this place. You think you can get away with firing off texts to people telling them to kill themselves? Think you can wither people with your condescending stares?"

The girls laughed.

"Let's keep it simple," Nakaya said, stepping up beside me. Her voice was incredibly calm. "Jade Cho is off limits. You even send her a kitten emoji and I'll kick your ass."

"It's a free world," the tall girl said. "We can talk to whoever we want. You're not the boss of us."

"Oh please," I said. I pulled up the modified Reducer, which was a silver cylinder, kind of like a wand. I aimed it at one of the girl's phones, then flicked it at all the other devices I could see. One after the other, the phones shrunk slightly, causing havoc inside their little smart phone bodies. I heard popping noises and the girls dropped their devices to the ground, smashing screens and cracking cases.

Nakaya pushed me back, cautious but still facing the girls.

"This is your only warning," she said.

"You're dead, Park," the girl said and launched forward, grabbing Nakaya's shirt. The other girls leapt at us too and I felt hands grabbing at me. Nakaya twisted her way out of the death-grip and shoved the tall girl back into Harriet. I backed away with a few scratches on my arms but otherwise unhurt.

"And now, the crying," I said softly. The girls were surrounding Nakaya, pushing at her, calling her names. I aimed the Reducer at Harriet first, targeting her trousers. The thin beam of light hit the grey pants and they tightened suddenly, pulling her out of her froth-mouthed curse. She grabbed at her waistline and I sent another beam of light at her shirt which tightened, buttons bursting. I fired off more shots at the girls, shrinking their clothes just enough to make it really uncomfortable. I was pretty impressed with the fine tuning. The Reducer had never been so subtle.

Nakaya stepped around the girls who were now all on their knees, pulling at their too-tight uniforms. Some other kids came closer, curious and a little bit cruel. I saw phones come out and pictures were taken.

Harriet was crying and so were the others, their

humiliation feeding on itself. They were like an adolescent mess of hormones and hatred.

I know it was just as bad as what they did to others. I'm not proud of making them look foolish, but sometimes I have to admit that I'm not this super-serious, super-brave, super-constructive teenager. I'm fourteen. I get annoyed sometimes, and I have this thing where I just hate bullies. So even if I become one for a flash of revenge, even if I take on the role of aggressor, it's petty and hateful but it's not all of me.

I can see it in Nakaya too. She's nasty sometimes, but there's stuff there behind those cool stares and those cutting words. Stuff with what people have said about her, her whole life. Stuff with trying to be someone that she probably doesn't want to be. I can relate. Harriet can relate. The whole whirling storm of girls we just wrecked can relate.

For me, my dad's missing. He's the size of a dog snack just waiting to happen. And I've got to hold everything together or else we'll break apart, my family will fall to dust, and we'll never get it back together again.

We all have reasons. We can all relate.

And besides, as I look back at the shrieks of Harriet and her girls struggling with their mis-sized uniforms, I can also say it's research. The Reducer was working again. Praise the Techno Gods.

"So you were doing Girls' Stuff?" Will asked as we walked up the hill to collect Luca. Nakaya tagged along with us instead of catching a lift home with her friends. She said she wanted to pick up her brother, but I could tell she wanted to talk about what we'd done to Harriet.

"Girls were involved, yes," I said.

"You terrorised them," Jade said softly. "Maddie and Tia had to go home and Harriet ended up in Sick Bay until her mum came and picked her up. You went too far, Charlie."

"There's no evidence," I said, marvelling at how flat my voice sounded. Will had snuck his hand into mine again, and apart from that warmth I felt ice cold. The phones were all broken. No film, no pictures. "It's just their word against ours, and who's going to believe Nakaya and I broke all their phones?"

"The Principal might," Jade said. "When she gets back from the city."

"Everyone knows those girls are trouble," Nakaya said. "The school won't do anything to us, and even if they did, who cares about detention?"

"What if they suspend you?" Jade said.

"I pay my debts," Nakaya said. I smiled at her, but it wasn't very convincing. As the day went on I felt more and more uncomfortable with what I'd done. Will tried to cheer me up by passing me a poem he'd written in Geography, but even the forced rhymes had only chased away the gloom for a little bit.

"I'll deal with whatever comes along," I said. "Just tell

me if you get any more texts."

"Sure, whatever," Jade said. "It's not that I don't appreciate it, Charlie. I just don't want to cause any trouble."

At the primary school gate one of the teachers stood with a clipboard and a far-away stare. She wasn't Luca's teacher, but I'd seen her around during pick-up. She smiled at us and then looked away, wistfully towards the bay. Will leaned against the wire fence and pulled me to him, grabbing me in a hug. It was nice, but sudden, and very public. I frowned up at him but he bent forward and rubbed our noses together lightly.

"You wanna go to the Skate Park after we take Luca home?" he asked.

Nakaya and Jade looked away. Embarrassment and joy had a fight in my stomach and the world lurched from one extreme to the next.

"Where's Taram?" Nakaya asked the teacher.

"Hmmm?"

"Taram Park. Has he left already?" Nakaya asked.

"Um, yes. He left about five minutes ago."

"Which way did he walk?"

"Sorry, not following you," the teacher said.

"Which. Way. Did. He. Walk?" Nakaya asked slowly.

"He didn't walk, silly. Your uncle picked him up."

"What uncle?" Nakaya looked back at me quickly but then faced the teacher. "I don't have an uncle."

"Maybe it was one of the other kids' uncles then," she said, although she did seem a little concerned - or confused.

"Is Luca Conti here?" I asked, disentangling myself from Will.

"No," she said simply. "Taram's uncle picked him up too. Yeah, he picked up a whole lot of kids."

"What?" Will asked. "When? What kind of car? What did this uncle look like?"

He fired off questions like the lead in a TV police procedural.

"Hmm, had a scruffy kind of beard. A little round in the middle, perhaps. Was driving a white van."

"Anything on the van?"

"Something on the side," she said. "Said he worked for a moving company."

"You didn't think that was a little strange?" I asked, heart beating fast.

"It's a small town."

"Have you called the police?" Nakaya demanded.

"Why?"

"I'm on it," Will said, and pulled out his mobile.

"What's going on?" Jade asked as we stepped back from the teacher who went on looking towards the water. "What am I missing here?"

"I think our brothers have been kidnapped," I said. "Let's go. I need to pick up a few things from home."

"What about the police?" Jade asked.

"They're on their way here," Will said.

"Let's leave Miss Daydream to figure things out. I need to get back to the apartment. There are some things that only I can do, and this is all my fault anyway."

"It's not your fault," Will said.

"Yeah, I think it is. Will, I need to show you something."

After running through the lagoon and up to the main street, the four of us collapsed on the couch in my apartment. Nakaya helped herself to drinks in the fridge, throwing cans of soft drink to the others while I pulled out the sports bag I'd been stashing my equipment in.

I pulled out the ray-gun base of the Medusa-Reducer and clicked on the Reducer cylinder. It whirred into life.

"Holy moly!" Will said, totally losing his cool. "This is amazing!"

"Is that a gun?" Jade asked slowly.

"It's the Medusa-Reducer," I said. "I made it. I'm kind of a mad scientist, like in the comics. My Dad knows a few people in the business and he's probably got us all into this mess. There's an old man running around stealing gold and booster seats and he's mixed up with Mara Monzote and probably Dan Galkin."

Will and Jade exchanged puzzled looks.

"Long story short…" I said.

"Eeew!"

Nakaya jumped up from the couch, spilling soft drink everywhere. She pulled at something in the cushions and brought out a squirming little bearded man. He was grabbing at the air, kicking and making a little growling sound.

Dad.

I launched across and took him from Nakaya, looking around for something to put him in.

"You've got a little demon guy," Will said, standing up, still impressed and getting more and more so as the day went on. "What's his name?"

"It's my Dad," I said. I grabbed a biscuit tin from the bench and dropped him in, pressing the metal lid down. There were no air holes but it'd hold him for the moment. "Where was I?"

"Long story short," Nakaya offered.

"Right," I said. "New story. Luca and Taram are missing. We need to find them. The old guy has some tough goons working for him. If you're coming with me you'll need to be ready for some weird stuff."

"Weird stuff?" Will said. "I am in. All the way, like … this is cool."

"If you're interested," Nakaya said. "Isagrim is listed as attached to a trucking company out on the ring road. Never seen it myself, but the internet doesn't lie."

She held out her phone and I saw the stylised Isagrim logo.

"We'll need wheels," I said.

"I've got my scooter outside," Will said.

"Let's call that Plan B," I said, smiling at him. "Plan A calls for a pregnant sister. Anyone have one of those?"

"I don't get it," Jade said.

"We're going to ask Josie for a ride," I said. "Meet downstairs in five minutes."

Will leapt out the door and rattled down the stairs

leaving Jade and Nakaya in the apartment with me.

"Shouldn't we wait for the police?" Nakaya said.

"You remember Saturday night?" I said. "That burglar wasn't an ordinary boy."

Nakaya nodded slowly.

"I'll go find Josie," Jade said, and ran out the door.

"If you can make things bigger and smaller, Conti. Why don't you bring your dad back?" Nakaya asked. She was watching me closely. I looked at the biscuit tin and frowned. I could bring him back. I was confident the Medusa-Reducer was in perfect condition. All it would take was a single beam and Dad would be back.

Only, I wasn't sure that was what we needed right now.

"It's complicated," I said slowly. I picked up scissors and jabbed them into the tin, breaking the metal to let in air. "We're not talking magic here."

The thing was, Dad always messed things up. Every time we did something, Dad would somehow make it go weird or seriously wrong. He couldn't even be trusted to get milk from the supermarket. Luca was missing now, and if Dad was Dad again, he'd insist on taking charge.

I couldn't risk it.

I couldn't risk Luca.

"I don't really care, you know?" Nakaya said.

"I know," I said, smiling faintly as I put Dad in the sports bag and zipped it up. "But thanks for not caring, Nakaya."

Will pulled up the garage door, letting it roll up with a thunderous finality, and revealing Josie Cho's pride and joy. It was a black Holden Astra with neon pink rims and a number plate CH0CH0. Josie made her way through the dumbstruck Will and Nakaya, beeping the security off and unlocking the doors.

"Are we gonna fit?" Will asked. He had brought a cricket bat for the adventure, and had strapped up his hands like a prize-winning boxer. Jade had brought along a meat cleaver and mirror shades. I'd assembled a motley band of heroes. Josie was amused but didn't say anything. To her, maybe we just looked like we were practising some cosplay trick-or-treating or something.

"It'll be fine," I said. I wasn't sure, but we didn't have time. "Get in."

Nakaya called shotgun without uttering a word, relegating Will, Jade and me to the back seat of the hatchback.

"Where are we headed?" Josie asked. "Circus isn't in town, so I might need some directions."

"Ring Road. A truck depot there," Jade called out.

"Why not?" said Josie with a shrug. She pulled down her shades and checked the mirrors. "Belts."

The little car reversed out into the street and Josie swung it around easily to face East. She looked over her shoulder and narrowed her eyes as Will fumbled to put on his seat belt.

"Belts, Chase."

"Sorry," he said.

"I'm all about safety here," Josie said, and accelerated. There was a white van outside the museum as we past, and I looked at Jade who looked back at me with wide eyes.

"Wait, stop!" we yelled together.

Chapter Sixteen
Plan B

THERE WAS SOMETHING wrong about the situation in front of the museum. For starters, the back doors of the van were wide open and it was getting filled with ancient artefacts and gold. It was Monday afternoon. Across the street, the police station was strangely peaceful.

After we piled out of the car, Will started swinging his cricket bat, waiting for someone to hit. Nakaya had her fists clenched too, ready to take it to whoever had abducted our brothers. Jade and Josie, on the other hand, looked a bit hesitant. They kept close to the car and tried not to look out of place.

The doors to the museum opened and the pencil-thin crony from Saturday struggled with a bust of some Aztec God. He walked to the van and tipped it into the back, rubbing his hands on his overalls as it fell with a soft thump against some opulent looking cushions. He turned around and saw us standing in the street.

"I never saw that in the gift shop," Will said. "I reckon you're nicking stuff, mate."

The man kept his eyes on me but edged to the museum entrance. I pulled out the Medusa-Reducer and flicked the power switch. It hummed loudly in the street.

"Stop moving," I said. "And tell us how many of you are inside."

"You do not have to threaten my men, Fraulein," the bearded man called as he stepped out into the street from the museum. He was wearing overalls too but also had a headset with microphone. "I am very interested in that machine you have built. Perhaps we can make an exchange, no? I take only a little more of this treasure and you give me the ray gun."

I lifted it and fired. This time I hit him square-on.

"How about we try this again?" he said, smirking through his bushy beard. "I take all the gold and you also give me all of your ray gun? You see, I am engineer also, and I have found the little secret to your shrinking, freezing gadget."

I fired again, but there was no effect.

Two more men came out of the museum carrying what looked like a sarcophagus. They ignored us and slid it into the back of the truck.

"Plan B?" Will asked.

I flicked the Medusa-Reducer to the shrinking ray.

"What was Plan B?" I asked, blasting off a beam that was supposed to shrink the bearded man. I watched as the beam of energy dissipated an inch from his round belly. There was some kind of force field in play. "I hate force fields," I mumbled.

"Plan B was Will's scooter, wasn't it?" Jade piped up from behind the car.

"Nah, this is Plan B," Will said, and stepped forward, swinging his bat. It connected with the side of the van, shattering the window. He swung again and dented the door.

"Are we beating up on the van now?" Nakaya asked. "How is that helpful?"

"No get-away," Will said and moved to the side mirrors, swinging madly. Two of the cronies followed him, but he was light on his feet and dodged their grabs, swinging again at the front grill.

"Plan B," I said, nodding. The bearded man stepped towards me and I noticed he was holding another of those little metal ball bearings in his hand. It was probably a flare. "Jade, give me your phone, now."

"I don't have a phone anymore," she said.

"Now, Jade," I called again, stepping back a bit to keep the old man at bay. "Throw it here."

Jade pulled out her phone and threw it at me. I caught it and held it in front of me like a shield. The old man stopped and scratched his head. I flicked the switch on the Reducer.

"Are you going to call the police?" he asked, mocking fear. "I am afraid that we have already dealt with the constabulary."

"No, this call is for you," I said. I threw the phone at his head, blasting it with the Medusa-Reducer, so as it spun towards the man it grew, and grew and grew. When it collided with his forehead there was a solid thump and the old man keeled over backwards.

Jade ran up to me, eyes wide as she looked at her phone which was now the size of a bodyboard. The man lay still, his faded blue eyes staring blankly up at the clouds above.

"Nice shot, Charlie," Josie said.

"You broke my screen," Jade said.

Will and Nakaya came around from the front of the van and stared at the stunned man on the ground. Nakaya's hair was ruffled and she'd lost the pink bow. Will looked a bit out of breath too, but there was no sign of the three cronies.

"Are you two okay?" Josie asked. "I mean…"

"Fine," Nakaya said. "They ran off that way," she added, hooking her thumb down the street.

"Kids are all inside," Will said, slinging the bat over his shoulder like it was a broad sword. "Amazing how easy it is to talk with bad guys."

Nakaya grinned.

"Go and check on your Dad," I said. "Something's happened to the station and he might need your help. "Jade and Josie, you should stay out here just in case. Nakaya and I can handle this."

"I said I owed you one, Conti," Nakaya said. "By my count I'm already up to three."

"Let's just get our brothers and go home," I said. "To our own places, I mean. Not like I want to move in with your family or anything."

"Oh God," Nakaya said and followed me into the museum.

It didn't take us long to follow the chanting and the weird incense-like smells coming from one of the exhibit rooms. We crept through the museum, retracing our steps from the morning, but with a growing sense of dread.

"Isn't that voice…?" Nakaya started, but then we looked into the room. It had probably been used to store packing boxes and shipping crates. There was no window. The floorboards were bare and rather nice looking if you didn't notice the lines of chalk and golden dishes with stubby candles.

Miss Monzote was chanting from across the room, pulling a strap around a little girl who sat serenely in a stolen booster seat. The chalk lines formed some kind of pentagram but it wasn't a normal five-pointed star. This one looked weird, but since we were standing in a museum of ancient Aztec relics I figured it probably had something to do with their gods. At each crossing point of the diagram was a booster seat. They were all different sizes and the kids inside were a wide range too, from little babies to my eight year old brother.

They all looked oddly peaceful. Not asleep, but lulled by something.

"They'd better be okay," I said, stepping into the room with Nakaya by my side. "Because if you've even given them a headache, your life is not going to be worth living, Monzote."

She turned around and sized us up.

"Don't be such a bore, Charlie," she said.

"But you're supposed to be the teacher," Nakaya said. "Why are you here with those... those kids? You're supposed to be home marking essays or something."

"Please," she said. "I have seniors to do that."

Miss Monzote snapped the child restraint into place and patted the little girl on the head. She quickly counted the thirteen occupied booster seats with her finger, pointing at each one as she mouthed the numbers.

"It's always better to have a few extras," Miss Monzote said. "You always hear about things like this going awry because of poor planning."

"Things like what?" I asked.

"Do you want a monologue?" Miss Monzote touched her tortoise amulet and walked the perimeter of her diagram. When she passed Luca I swallowed hard. He looked like he had just eaten a huge dinner and was spacing-out on the Playstation.

Miss Monzote stepped over the line and walked to the centre where a box sat on a low stool. She lifted the box and revealed a skull with red gemstones in the eye sockets. It sat on the top of the flat vase I'd seen her with in the restaurant. She tossed the box away, over the heads of the children.

"Shall I simply show you instead?"

I raised the Medusa-Reducer.

"Maybe I should just stop you right there," I said.

"Grim told me about your little toy, Charlie, dear. He's rigged up these little repulsor fields to keep us safe. I'm surprised he didn't tell you himself - he's been so vocally impressed with himself all morning."

"Is everyone here a supervillain?" Nakaya said, rolling her eyes. "Let's just call the police and get Taram out of here."

"No one's getting out of here, Nakaya. Except maybe her." She pointed to the flat vase which sat under the skull. "She's been waiting an awfully long time, but now I've found a way to bring her back."

"You're raising a dead Aztec mummy?" Nakaya asked. "This is seriously bad form, Conti. Only when you turn up does everything go weird. Couldn't you have just stayed away in the city?"

"This is my fault?" I asked, looking incredulously at Nakaya who folded her arms and stared back with daggers in her eyes.

"It's no one's fault," Miss Monzote said. "But here, you can help me a little by screaming."

Nakaya and I stopped staring at each other and turned back to our teacher who was holding a sleek black pistol. Looked like a Kimber 9mm. I know pistols. Never touch them myself but it's been kind of a family interest since I was little.

I expected her to threaten us some more, or walk up and down like a lioness, but she squeezed the trigger and fired two shots into the roof.

Nakaya ducked to the floor, crouching, afraid. The kids screamed, suddenly aware of their surroundings and petrified. I stepped back and hit the wall, my heart racing. This was no time to panic.

"My beloved Chalchiuhtlicue is protector of children," Miss Monzote said, walking towards me around the diagram. "When she hears their cries, she will come. She will step out into this world and I shall be here to show her the greatness, the madness of this place."

I gritted my teeth.

"You want to be a tour guide for a goddess?" I asked, and then launched at her, grabbing the tortoise amulet from around her neck with one hand and shoving her backwards with my shoulder. The twisting action snapped the chain and I had the amulet but no Miss Monztoe. She fell to the ground and let loose another bullet which lodged into the wall behind me.

I wasn't sure she meant to fire at me. Her eyes looked surprised. She hesitated.

So I went for the gun. I kicked it out of her hand and across the floor, but the History teacher grabbed my foot and pulled me off-balance, bringing me down on the ground with her. I rolled away but she held on to my leg.

"No one can even pronounce the stupid name," I said, kicking again.

"They will…" Monzote panted hard, crawling away from me. "… learn her name."

The kids' screams were getting worse. I saw Nakaya trying to get her brother out of his harness and then I saw Dad leaping around. Somehow he'd got out of my bag. He was running like a leprechaun towards the skull with the pretty gems. I shouldn't have been surprised.

I launched myself at him, skidding across the floor, hopefully smudging the chalk lines to disrupt whatever it was Miss Monzote was doing. My hand stretched out and I grabbed my little father, pulling him away from the skull. I sat up and looked at him, at his wildly flailing arms and legs.

"Oh Dad," I said. He squawked at me.

There was a strange sound beyond the kids' screams. Miss Monzote had pulled herself together enough to get back to the centre of the diagram too, and I sat there watching her lift the skull. Her hair was standing on end, swaying about in some invisible, mystical wind. I felt my own hair rise and knew something bad was about to happen.

"She will be here soon," Miss Monzote said and picked up the vase, lovingly staring at it. At least the gun was gone. "She will be here soon."

There was a movement at the door and I looked around to see Dan Galkin skid through, looking worried and then confused. The way his face shifted from one emotion to the next was almost comical.

"You're late," Miss Monzote said.

"There's … ah … people outside. Couldn't get through easily."

"What are you doing here?" I yelled, standing up. I squeezed Dad in my hand to keep him from escaping and backed out of the diagram towards the Medusa-Reducer. It might not have worked on these people but I had a way of getting around that. I could find my way around a stupid repulsor field.

"Do it," Miss Monzote said.

Dan nodded and raised his hands parallel with the floor. Blue light circled his hands and up his arms, coiling around like snakes. Little flashes of white light burst along the chalk lines and suddenly the room was awash with electrical fire. It leapt up along the lines and Dan was conducting it somehow, waving his hands slightly, bringing it under control.

Damn kid was an uberhuman.

I should have guessed earlier, and maybe I did. There are some people born with unusual and inhuman powers. They're called uberhumans, after some ancient German philosophy book. It doesn't matter. There are some good ones like most of the Celestial Knights, but there are a lot of bad ones too.

I was putting Dan into that category now.

Miss Monzote raised the vase with fully extended arms and an insane smile plastered across her smug face. The kids still screamed. Nakaya was crying, pulling at her brother's restraints. Dad started biting me, but I found the Medusa-Reducer and gripped it tightly. Then Miss Monzote smashed the vase down hard against the floor.

It shattered.

Chapter Seventeen
The Goddess With
The Impossible Name

I KNOW IT'S probably a surprise to everyone, but I've never met a goddess before. Sure, I've had more than my fair share of encounters with mad scientists and costumed crazies, but none of them have actually had any kind of real claim to godhood.

This goddess was perspiring designer water from her pores, all sparkling and streaming in rivulets down her strangely longer than normal limbs. And where her bare feet touched the museum floor, I kid you not, small green plants just shot up. Right through the floor of the museum.

It didn't make sense. It wasn't rational.

And that's why I knew she was a real-to-crazy goddess.

Miss Monzote called her Chalchiuhtlicue.

It didn't matter that I couldn't pronounce it. It didn't matter that no one else on the entire planet could pronounce it. She was trouble.

She had grown out of the shattered vase, impossible waves of liquid rolling out of the small pottery pieces until it grew into a towering woman. Waves of white ice hair, dark markings on her skin. At first she just stood there, her body rippling with movement, but without actually moving from the spot she had formed in. Miss Monzote knelt before her, arms outstretched, pleading with the goddess in some unknown language.

The kids' screams intensified, which I know sounds impossible, but when something like that happens and you're stuck in a booster seat, you would lose your cool too.

Chalchiuhtlicue focused on the kids. Her too-wide eyes got even bigger and her face smoothed out like water washing away any confusion. She reached out to a girl, her arms growing so she got closer without moving her feet. The arms stretched and then the fingers.

The girl's face was covered in tears but she stopped screaming at the goddess' touch.

I lifted the Medusa-Reducer, but then Dan skidded beside me, pushing the pistol down, sitting next to me and huddled close. His face was bruised. He looked exhausted.

The booster seat snapped open as Chalchiuhtlicue's fingers dissolved into a stream of water which rolled over the girl and through the seat. Her arm re-formed and she picked up the girl, bringing her back to her bosom. Like, literally back to her chest, nursing her like a baby. The girl was probably only a year younger than Luca.

The goddess reached out ten more arms, forming them out of the reservoirs of her unnatural body, freeing the other children and bringing them back to her.

Nakaya grabbed at Taram when his seat clicked open, but Chalchiuhtlicue simply knocked her back with a blast of ice-water, drenching Nakaya and knocking her into the wall. Taram reached out for his sister but the goddess' will was stronger and he was dragged to her embrace.

I pushed against Dan, trying to get free from his clumsy hold, but he kept me down.

"Wait," he said, close. "It's dangerous."

"Have it," I said, shoving the Medusa-Reducer at him and scrambling back to my feet. The kids were being pulled into the goddess' watery body, submerging their screams, pacifying them. I saw Luca disappear into her body and ran towards him, forgetting about Dad, forgetting about weapons, forgetting about everything except for my little brother.

Chalchiuhtlicue was huge but I leapt towards her face, surprised by the spring in my step. The tortoise amulet was still in my hand and I swung it into a punch, colliding with the goddess' face. I felt the impact ripple outward and saw her face shift into a featureless well of liquid. She had grabbed me though, somehow extending her body to trap me up to my waist. We were eye to eye, if she had eyes, so I punched her again, using the amulet to strike the liquid.

"Hold her there!" yelled Miss Monzote. I thought she was yelling at me but Dan stood up and blasted Chalchiuhtlicue with lightning, keeping a steady stream of energy coursing into the goddess.

Miss Monzote laughed.

Remember when I told you that I'd never met a goddess before? It's true, but I have had my fair share of megalomaniacs. When Miss Monzote let loose on her wild cackle I knew what I had to do. Whenever there's something too powerful, too all-encompassing to overcome, you go for the strings.

In this case, I knew Miss Monzote was somehow pulling the strings on Chalchiuhtlicue. It might have been something to do with Dan's weird blue lightning or maybe it was the child-like chalk drawings. Whatever it was, I knew that if I could take out Miss Monzote we might have a chance against the goddess.

I struggled.

Even though I'd landed two blows against Chalchiuhtlicue's face with the tortoise amulet, she still had a good hold of my lower body inside her gelatinous, weird syrupy torso. I pushed away from her but my hands got stuck. I looked inside the semi-transparent body and saw little kids floating around like chocolate frogs in jelly. Their eyes were wide, their mouths open in silent screams.

It wasn't encouraging.

I reached my hand further into the liquid body which brought my face way too close to Chalchiuhtlicue. I could smell her, like really old water left in the kitchen sink. Earthy. Definitely on the nose.

I had no idea what was happening behind me but Chalchiuhtlicue was still lashing out around the room, grabbing kids and slapping the walls with her octopus-like arms. I stretched my arm to my leg, pushing through the body. And then, when I had a hold, I pushed my leg outward which was incredibly difficult. I felt like I was doing a tumble roll in really slow motion.

There wasn't any way to completely free my leg, though,

unless I wanted to duck my head inside Chalchiuhtlicue. Miss Monzote moved around to the perfect spot, looking up to the beatific/mad face of her goddess. I sighed.

Another sacrifice.

I rolled my body, tipping my top half inside the goddess while shoving my leg out. It really was like dunking yourself in a bucket of grimy washing water, but as soon as my leg was free I kicked out hard and connected with Miss Monzote's face.

She went down.

No more laughing.

But there was no more me, either. With an oddly distant slurping sound I felt my leg get sucked back inside and I watched, helplessly, as Chalchiuhtlicue collected the last of the kids, as well as Dan and Nakaya whose face had shown absolute revulsion at the goddess' touch. I thought it was over. We were all going to be dissolved inside the alien stomach of an ancient goddess.

No one would have believed me if I'd told them back home in the city. Sure, there were bets on around the docklands about how we'd all meet our ends. Zali and Anise, who were my on-again, off-again besties, dreamed up all kinds of demises but mostly they involved birds eating your eyeballs or plagues of gnomes marching you off to a giant compost to be buried alive and used later for garden mulch.

Honestly, I thought I'd live a long life.

The inside of the goddess was soothing though. Everything seemed so detached and it was warm and there was a gentle pressure around you, like a mother's hug. I felt myself getting drowsy.

There was the distant sound of drums and the call of exotic birds.

I closed my eyes.

Chapter Eighteen
The Near Death Dining Experience

WE'RE SITTING AT the dinner table, only it's from the house we lived in when I was just a little kid. The table is sleek and black and soul-less. It stretches a long way and I can't see either end. I'm dressed in my black jacket and I'm fourteen still, but everything else looks out of time.

Next to me, Luca is licking a bowl with a thin, darting tongue. He's chasing a couple of flies around the bowl, tipping it so they fall to one side and then tipping it the other way. His ears have flattened against his skull and he looks a little weird. I tip the chair back a bit and notice he has a tail.

Across from me sits my mother.

She is wearing an elegant black cocktail dress. Her neck looks so regal, so long and thin, and her eyes are watching me. They are black. Beside her sits the goddess, Chalchiuhtlicue. She's wearing a gigantic feather head-dress and her chest is wrapped in bandages, but designed to look rather stylish. She's also looking at me, but I see hunger in her eyes.

It's a dream.

"I will look after you now," Chalchiuhtlicue says, but

her mouth isn't moving. It's still stuck in a rictus smile, and the words echo around the darkened dream-room. "I will look after all the children."

"Mum?" I ask, reaching my hands across to her. She still watches me from above, her head cocked as if she can't believe I'm really there, and isn't sure she is pleased about it. "Mum, can't you do something?"

"I am your 'mum' now," Chalchiuhtlicue says. She reaches out for my hands but I pull them back, knocking Luca as I do so. He leaps back in surprise, twisting, shifting into something else. His legs bend, his body stretches and he's a lizard. I stand up, pushing my chair away, but he's gone, scuttling away into the shadows.

I turn back to Mum. She is still seated, but Chalchiuhtlicue has stood up and is slowly making her way on to the table itself, pawing ahead of her like a cat. Her body is elongated, unnatural.

She is hunting me.

"Mum? Say something."

My mother turns her head slightly so she is looking directly at me. Her dark eyes blink and her lips part.

"What is there to say, Charlie?" she asks. "I think we've done enough talking."

"We haven't even said anything," I shout. "You never say anything."

"That's because I'm not here," she says.

"And who's fault is that!?"

My mother smiles - just a little twitch at the corner of her mouth.

"You made your choice," she says.

"And you made yours," I say. I reach forward and grab the edge of my empty plate, tipping it at the advancing Chalchiuhtlicue. The clanging noise startles the goddess and she squats on the table, licking at her long fingers. There's blood on them, like chocolate syrup.

"You're not a child anymore, Charlie," my mother says.

"I am, Mum, I am still a child," I say. I can feel more words inside me: hateful, angry, horrible words; but I can't bring them out. I can barely speak. My throat tightens and I think I'm going to cry.

"We all have to make sacrifices," my mother says.

"I will be your mummy," Chalchiuhtlicue's voice echoes around the room. "Come to the warm place, the place of light and the water of life. Come with me to the paradise place, where we shall welcome worshippers together."

The walls of the dark room shimmer and I see glimpses of rainforest out of the corners of my eyes. I hear more sounds, distant but crystal clear. Birds and water and laughter, too, somewhere off a little.

"You think we're in South America," I say softly. I catch another twist of my mother's smile. "You want us to go back with you."

"We are already there," the voice whispers all around me.

"No we're not," I say. "We're still in Henty Bay, and you have no idea what you've brought yourself into."

I am in control here.

I reach into the shadows under the table and pull out

a larger version of the Medusa-Reducer, forming it out of the dream stuff. It looks incredibly powerful and a little bit sinister if I'm honest. Chalchiuhtlicue reaches behind her and pulls out two long ice daggers.

"Oooo, let us play," her voice says, purring like a cat.

She launches herself at me from the table, pushing us back so I stumble against the shadowy walls and then all the way through them. Suddenly we're not having dinner, but instead we're surrounded by lush green forest. It's full of smooth-leaved plants and thin, tremulous trees and an overwhelming heat.

I dance around a tree as the goddess lunges at me with her daggers. She swishes one in the air and a storm of ice blasts outward, coating the tree I'm hiding behind with a sheet of frozen water. She swishes again and more ice comes out, slicing the tree and bringing it down. I leap away and keep low, letting the lower bushes obscure my escape. Birds fly over head in streaks of colour. I look up and see a bird with feathers of rainbow fire.

None of it's real.

"You will help me find the path home," Chalchiuhtlicue coos, creeping behind me, following the path I've made in the ferns. "And we shall return to the paradise place."

I swing the Medusa-Reducer back towards her voice but I can't see her. I can hear her, no problem, but all around me is a forest of green.

"You're not supposed to be in this time," I call out. I feel an icy breeze to my left and swing around but she's not there. "No one knows you here."

"They shall learn my name again."

The voice comes from above and I swing my gun up at the trees, but it's a ruse, and Chalchiuhtlicue grabs me from a different direction, knocking the Medusa-Reducer to the ground. She grabs my neck and raises her hand to strike with the dagger.

"None of this is real," I say, struggling against her choke hold. "It's just a way to keep from facing the truth."

She tilts her head sideways, intrigued.

"I've been hiding in here for years," I say. "It might be your rain forest, but it's my mind. You're nothing in here."

I reach for the Medusa-Reducer and feel my fingers take hold.

Chalchiuhtlicue hesitates again, and her face shifts like water running over a window. I see her features still, her hungry eyes and stretched smile; but behind the grotesque mask is my mother. I can see her dark eyes watching me. She isn't smiling. She never really did even when she was around.

"I know what I have to do," I say to my mother.

She nods slightly.

I lift the gun and pull the trigger.

Chapter Nineteen
The End Game

HAVE YOU EVER gone swimming in your clothes? The first thing I saw was the road: wet, dark and hard. My hair was hanging in front of me, thick with the gelatinous goo that had been the goddess. My chest was heaving, trying to breathe in the delicious air. And I was outside. I could feel the sun on the back of my head as I held myself up on my knees, hands pressing into the road.

I wasn't dead.

I sat up slowly, running my hands back to untangle my hair and wipe away the remains of Chalchiuhtlicue. The street outside the museum was an interesting mix of bystanders and kids. Babies were crying, little kids were throwing bits of the goo at each other and to my right was the unconscious bearded man I now knew was called Grim. It fitted him rather nicely.

"Are you okay?" asked Will, kneeling beside me. He had his cricket bat close by and it looked like it'd been busy. Alongside the cherry marks from the cricket ball there were dents in the wood that could only have come from hitting a white van. "I mean, you look terrible, but are you okay?"

"You're a keeper," I said, giving him a quick smile. He

stood up and offered me his hand, which I took gratefully and heaved myself to my feet. Nakaya was nearby, drenched but hugging her little brother. Jade and Josie were leaning against the Astra, and Mr and Mrs Cho had emerged from the restaurant and were helping people in off the street. Parents came running from all directions to collect their children. Some high school kids even pitched in, herding sad, disoriented boys and girls into the comic shop where they called parents and guardians.

"What happened?" I asked.

"She blew up," Will said. "She came bursting out here waving these watery tentacle things around and screaming. Looked like a trifle, actually, with all you guys inside."

Jade ran over and hugged me.

"Oh my God you're gross," she said, hugging me tighter. "It was horrible," she said, pulling back and grinning. "We had the old man covered but Will couldn't get into the police station. It's locked. No one can phone in or anything."

"I'm not worried," Will said. "Sarge is pretty resourceful."

"Oh God," I said, suddenly freaking out. "Where's my Dad?"

Luca trudged up to us holding a soaked backpack. His fringe was covering his eyes and he looked seedy, like he'd eaten too much junk food.

"I got him," he said in a croaky voice. "Can we go home now?"

Clouds covered the sun and the street felt chilly. It wasn't just me who felt it. Parents quickly dragged their kids away and some shop keepers slammed their doors like in an old Western. I looked at the road and saw the globs of jelly-like goddess start to move.

I shook off the bigger globs from my clothes as they shuddered back towards the middle of the street. All around me, other people were freaking out as most of the goo came to life.

"Uh-oh," Jade said. "This can't be good."

From all over the street, Chalchiuhtlicue started to pull herself together. The jelly was darker, full of grit and dirt. It heaved towards the centre, moving faster and faster in lurching movements, leaving the road slick and dangerous. I held my footing but only just. Luca grabbed hold of my leg and I stood there watching an Aztec goddess re-form out the front of Culture Kit.

It wasn't pretty.

Chalchiuhtlicue was larger now, towering over us in a sloppy form that showed none of her grace and none of her beauty. She was an angry, molten mess and shrieked through five mouths which formed even as the sound reverberated around the town centre. She was truly hideous.

The two owners of Culture Kit raced inside as she swung her tentacles in a flurry of pain and frustration. The water-fists smashed into walls and windows, overturned cars and upended a tree. We all hit the road, cowering together and hoping for a nicer mood swing. I figured there was a small chance she'd just stomp off into Henty Bay and swim back to South America.

The cries of children brought her to her senses, or at least tugged her in the right direction. I noticed her head swivel, trying to pin-point the pain and fright she heard.

There were plenty of kids crying, so it wasn't difficult to find one that needed her attention. And that was what Chalchiuhtlicue was all about. She wanted to protect all the children. Of course, by protecting them, she was actually trying to ingest them in her goddess jelly-belly. We couldn't let that happen.

There was a flash of lightning. It arced through the street starting out low and then shooting up and through the goddess' head. Dan Galkin stood in front of Chalchiuhtlicue, clad in his motor-cross body armour. He was glowing a faint blue and electricity was jumping at him from all around. He was sucking it in from the parked cars, from shop lighting, from the power lines. With every pulse of energy I could almost see his skeleton, and for the first time in a very long time, I was scared.

People like Dan were dangerous, unpredictable. Living bombs.

He reached his arms forward and his whole body convulsed, pushing the power he had absorbed through his outstretched arms and into Chalchiuhtlicue. The thunderstrike shattered the windows all along the street and blew off chunks of the goddess.

Dan drew in his breath and threw a second strike at her.

"She's made of water," Luca shouted. "Turn her into mud or something!"

I nodded, my brain running through a whole bunch of scenarios. None of them seemed to end with a happy ever after. I focused, pulling in the scene, counting assets, discounting liabilities. I had a lot of friends here: Jade, Will,

Josie, even Nakaya. I just needed to join the dots and come up with a plan.

Another thunderclap snapped me out of my planning space-out.

It was there all along, just like most good plans.

"This might work," I said, grabbing Luca and pulling him closer. "You get the kids out of the street. We need to clear the place because this might get even worse."

He nodded.

"I'll take them to Momma Cho," he said, saluting me and running off.

I turned to Jade. She had her hands clapped over her ears and was watching Dan go toe-to-toe with the goddess. I could tell he was losing it, though. The energy wasn't burning as bright and Chalchiuhtlicue was still the size of our apartment.

"I need you to set a trap," I said to Jade. "We need to get Chal...choo... what's her name, the goddess, into the supermarket." I told Jade the plan and after the slightest of pauses she nodded seriously and ran back to Josie at the Astra.

I looked around for the Medusa-Reducer and saw a random kid holding it. Part of me panicked but I walked towards him as calmly as possible, holding out my hand. He looked up at me and smiled wide-eyed. Slowly he held it up to me and I took it.

"You're a super hero," he said.

"Something like that," I said. I checked the gauges and the power levels seemed to be stable. "Now, go and get yourself off the street. Maybe hunker down in the comic shop."

He nodded and ran off.

Chalchiuhtlicue slammed Dan back towards me, thumping him with the force of a tidal wave. He skidded along the asphalt, tumbling over until he came to a stop at my feet.

He groaned and then looked up at me. His blonde hair was flat against his head, covering his eyes. I knelt down and parted it, getting a little electric shock as I touched him. Chalchiuhtlicue stretched towards the supermarket, scooping up a couple of kids who hadn't had the brains to get out of sight.

"You got hit in the face again," I said, wincing a bit as I saw the cuts and bruises around his eyes and lip. He shrugged and pulled himself up a bit, although he wasn't ready to stand.

"It doesn't matter," he said. "Not dead yet."

"You are a jerk, Dan."

He nodded.

"Fair call, that."

"I need you to help finish this," I said. "I'm going to cause a distraction, get her to follow me, but at the end I'll need your lightning god powers, okay?"

"You saw that, huh?" He tried to pull himself up a bit, but I could tell he was still in pain.

"Yeah, it was hard to miss."

"Okay, no problem."

We stood up together and I saw Will watching us from the chemist. He looked hurt, standing there drenched in his tank top. His cricket bat was gone but he wasn't hiding. He was just standing there as the goddess raged towards him.

It was like he already knew the plan.

I ran across the street, pushing myself harder to get under the waterfalls of Chalchiuhtlicue's legs. I was completely drenched so it didn't matter that I ended up with a few more buckets of goddess on my head. Will saw me and looked worried as I ran under the giant. He reached out for me and I grabbed his hand, letting him pull me close to the chemist window.

The goddess scooped up more bystanders, bringing them into her body as she wailed around the street. I wanted to finish it, but Will was holding me still. His eyes darted from left to right, hands holding my face, searching for any injury. I blinked and then he bent in and kissed me, pressing his lips against mine, holding my head against his. My arms reached out and grabbed his waist.

What a kiss.

I pulled back and looked into his eyes. There was no time for another plan.

"Sorry for this," I said.

I pushed him backward, hooked my foot behind his and flipped him through the display table at the front of the chemist. He crashed through the make up and toiletries perfectly, yelling out a surprised cry as he broke the table. I leapt over him and into the seat of a mobility scooter, starting it up and hoping it had some grunt.

Will sat up in the middle of the debris, shock evident on his face.

"It gets worse," I said.

"Why'd you do that?"

"You be the bait," I said. "And try to scream loud, okay?"

I undid the lame security cord that kept the scooters tethered to each other and quickly hooked it around Will's ankle. It was slippery with the goddess' jelly, just like everything else. I flipped the scooter into forward and heaved the machine out of the doors, turning quickly to head to the supermarket next door. Will screamed behind me as his body banged along the pavement. If it wasn't for the layer of goo that covered everything, things could have been bloody. Instead, it was sort of like a slightly dangerous slip'n'slide.

Chalchiuhtlicue was towering over us and she couldn't ignore the pain of a kid in distress. She reached out for Will who screamed louder as her tentacles stretched out for him. He waved his arms, covering his face just as we slid in through the automatic doors of the supermarket. I kept driving as Chalchiuhtlicue slammed up against the doors which stopped her for a few seconds. She concentrated her power into the multitude of arms, discharging the kids who had been encased inside her body. As they plopped safely to the pavement outside the supermarket the goddess smashed her way inside, inundating the place with her monstrous form.

Will fishtailed behind the scooter and I pulled him free as the goddess surged forward. Will grabbed on to me as the waves pushed us further into the store and I held on to him while also navigating us towards aisle 8. Most customers jumped out of the way of the deluge, but some got stuck and joined in our washing machine run towards the pet food section.

The water receded, pulling itself back into the form of Chalchiuhtlicue who looked more humanoid this time. Her feather head-dress flowed beautifully and her skin was a less murky-brackish colour and more a tanned human colour.

"I grow tired," her voice rolled over us from all directions. There was sadness there, and fatigue. Dan's fireworks show must have hurt her. "Give me the babies."

Will freaked out and pulled me to my feet again, slopping our way up the aisle. He kept himself between me and the goddess, pushing me along, breathing hard. I saw Jade and Josie up ahead. The End Game.

The two Cho girls were standing on huge bags of Alley Cat kitty litter. Jade had sliced open the bags with her cleaver and the crystals were strewn across the laminated floor. Josie stood on top of the pile, swinging Will's cricket bat. Between them they had demolished most of the store's supply of kitty litter.

As Will and I made it to the edge of the kitty litter hill we stopped and turned to face Chalchiuhtlicue. Behind us, Josie swung the cricket bat menacingly. For a pregnant woman she looked kick-ass.

"You think you look after all the babies?" she called out. "Well, you can't have mine."

"Ah… supreme mother of unborn child…" the voice floated around us. Chalchiuhtlicue's face shifted again as she saw Josie standing on top of the mound. Her arms reached out, cradling the imagined baby in her hands. Josie stayed her ground, eyes narrowed, her hands gripping the bat.

"Now might be a good time," I called to Dan who was walking slowly up behind her. He'd made it to the chew toys. "This is it!"

Dan pulled the electricity from around him again, draining the row of registers out front and blowing the lights up and down the store. It all flew into him as I levelled the Medusa-Reducer and fired off a concentrated beam. Dan's lightning shot through the back of Chalchiuhtlicue's head and she screamed.

The effects of the Reducer were agonisingly slow. At first she started to shimmer and the hole in her watery head was steaming but unable to re-form. Dan started to channel more electricity into her body in regular pulses, while I pulled even harder on the trigger willing it to work. The kitty letter crystals pulled at her as well, absorbing her liquid, trapping her in place. She writhed and a haunting wail filled the supermarket.

"Charlie!" Luca called out from the end of the aisle. I could see him through the wavering goddess. He had my backpack strapped on and in his hands he held a fire extinguisher.

"Don't think that's going to help," I called back.

Chalchiuhtlicue shuddered again and then pulled into herself, wrapping her arms around her body, once, twice and even more. She started to spin and shifted from a goddess into a water spout. Luca ran up to us but he was on the other side with Dan, who was still glowing like a radioactive mutant.

The Medusa-Reducer shuddered too.

"Give me some juice, Dan!" I yelled out. "Fire it into the converter at the front."

Dan shook his head, still firing at the water spout with his lightning.

"We're not going to do it unless we shrink her," I called out. "I need you! Fire the energy into the converter!"

The forked lightning changed direction, hooking around in mid-air, hopefully controlled by Dan. It condensed into a single bolt and hit the convertor at the end of the Reducer. I held on tight even as I felt the whole thing surge. It was nearly too hot to hold, but I pressed my fingers harder down on the trigger.

The kitty litter held her in place and Dan's electricity disrupted her corporeal form. In my hasty but valid calculations, the Reducer should have been able to do the rest of the job and obliterate her into nothingness. But something was wrong.

The beam from the Reducer started to pulse a dangerous red. I'd never seen it do that before, but it seemed to be working. Chalchiuhtlicue shrunk. The spinning water twisted itself into a pocket-sized version, and then even smaller.

Josie and Jade leapt into action, pushing more of the kitty litter onto the rapidly shrinking goddess. Will and Luca joined in, kicking and scooping. I lifted the beam and released the trigger, taking out a few shelves of cat products before I realised it wasn't turning off. I aimed it at the roof, which was a really bad idea, and the whole thing shrunk into a cascading mess of plaster.

"It's gonna blow!" Luca shouted and grabbed for the gun,

slinging off the backpack as he did so. I pulled it away from him, out of reach, but in doing so I swung the beam to take out more of the roof. Luca fell on his backside, arms covering his eyes as parts of the roof fell. I held the beam as steady as I could but I could feel myself crying I looked down at him, so vulnerable. He peeked through his fingers, surrounded by a horde of miniature cat and dog toys. My little brother was right. There was no way the Medusa-Reducer was going to survive so much power. I held on to it, hoping it would end quickly, closing my eyes.

I felt the heat of Dan before I saw him, probably because my eyes were so shut up. He held my hands and then gently took the gun away. When I did look again I saw him holding it straight down so it wouldn't shrink anything else, and it was slowing down. The charge seemed to dim, the power running back into Dan.

In a blink it was over.

Dan dropped the spent Medusa-Reducer on the floor and stepped back, shaking his head as if to clear vertigo. He stumbled a bit but seemed okay. I gave the gun a tentative tap from my boot but it was totally inert.

"She's adorable," Jade said.

Tearing herself away from the kitty litter crystals, which wouldn't let go of her, Chalchiuhtlicue looked like a very angry fairy. I grabbed my backpack and pulled out the snow dome Will had given me, kneeling down next to the mound and twisting the base. It cracked and some of the syrupy liquid poured out over my fingers, but I kept most of it in. I picked up Chalchiuhtlicue and dropped her inside.

"Wait!" Luca called and skidded beside me. He lifted a miniaturised squeaky pig toy and dropped it inside the dome. "She's lonely."

"Um, okay," I said, and closed the lid over the goddess, twisting it tight. Luca pulled out some packing tape from my backpack. I gave him a smile and sealed the snow dome, biting off the end of the tape and tossing it back in the bag.

"Is that going to hold her?" Will asked.

"For now," I said.

"She's doing a little dance," Luca said, taking the dome from me and giving it a bit of a shake so the snow started falling all around the little goddess. The squeaky pig looked like it was doing somersaults and Chalchiuhtlicue reached out to it, cradling it even as she tumbled end over end in a flurry of glitter flakes.

"So's your Dad," Will said. "Look."

Dad had crawled up the side of the kitty litter hill and was lying on his back doing a good impression of a snow angel, waving his arms and legs and having a great time. I went to pick him up but he was in such a good mood that I let him be. The Medusa-Reducer was broken again so I had no way of bringing him back to Dad-size.

Dan stumbled down the aisle to the exit. He didn't look very good. Other people were coming into the supermarket, cautiously gawking and talking to each other. They let Dan pass and he didn't look back.

"We'd better get home," I said.

Chapter Twenty
Our Happy Ever After
(With Popcorn)

FRIDAY NIGHT CRAWLED around, and after four days of stares and questions and even TV crews from Melbourne, Henty Bay had started to settle down. Classes had been cancelled on the Tuesday and I'd spent the day in my pyjamas watching daytime TV with Luca and Dad, who was still shrunk, but he'd stopped trying to escape. It was mostly because we'd put him back in the jar, but we'd sat it next to the snow dome and he liked looking at the dancing goddess. She was probably just jumping around the dome cursing me but when you gave it a little shake and the snow swirled around it really did look like she was dancing.

Jade and I caught up again on Wednesday but we didn't talk about the museum or Miss Monzote. The Walrus took us for history and he told us we didn't need to complete the project on the Aztecs. We moved straight into studying Federation which was a nice, dull topic with very little chance of anything going wrong. Will started sitting beside me in class, and even though his friends laughed and teased him, he stuck with me and walked me home. Most of the time we held hands.

Dan hadn't come back to school. Will told me his dad went over to the Galkin house to ask questions but he wasn't there. Apparently Dan disappeared for weeks at a time and nobody seemed to care, least of all his Mum. Nakaya kept her distance but she smiled at me at the canteen so that was something. And Taram drew a picture of me fighting Chalchiuhtlicue, although I looked more like one of the comic book heroes than a real girl. He even put me in a skirt and cape. Kid has imagination.

Good news is that the man called Grim is in custody. After Will's Dad and the other policemen escaped their station, they picked up Grim and his associates. Miss Monzote had disappeared and Dan seemed a bit beyond the police at the moment, but at least Grim would get some time in prison.

And then it was Friday and Jade invited me to Will's house for a movie night. Will didn't mind. His Dad was working late, again, going through paperwork and the phone calls he still seemed to have to make. His Mum was at a book club meeting and his two older brothers had locked themselves in their bedrooms listening to loud music or playing on their consoles. We had the place to ourselves.

Luca and I left Dad at Mrs Cho's place and she gave him a bowl of prawn crackers which he was happy to play in and munch on when the mood took him. I'd promised myself that I would start work on the Reducer over the weekend but it was going to take a lot of work.

Will's house was pretty nice, but it looked like it was full of teenage boys. Football boots hung by the front door and you had to step over tumbled scooters to get to the kitchen. There were photographs of his older brothers and their sporting trophies all over the living room. Will brought out some toys for Luca to play with and stacked half a dozen movies on the low lying coffee table in front of the couch. Jade kicked off her shoes and looked through them, fanning them out over the surface.

"Rom-com, horror, horror, animation… Have you got anything recent?" Jade asked.

"I thought we could watch an oldie," he said. "What about Nightmare on Elm Street?"

"What about 'No'!" Jade said, but I laughed so Will took that as a yes. He clicked open the cover and slipped the DVD into the machine. Jade rolled her eyes and went to the kitchen.

"Popcorn," I said as Will came back to sit on the couch, dropping himself right next to me so our legs touched. He stretched his arm along the back of the couch and stared at me, his dopey smile hinting at something a little more flirty.

"You're my hero," he said softly and bent in to kiss me. I held up my hand and he ploughed his lips against my palm, kissing loudly and a little wetly. I pulled back and frowned at him, trying not to laugh as I wiped his slobber over his shirt. "No kiss?"

"I don't know," I said. He leaned in again but stopped close to my face, forcing me to look into his eyes. They sparkled. He was so cute, so clean and good. Even his hair smelled good.

"I think I love you, Charlie Conti," he said, but I turned away. He sighed and I could feel his warm breath against my cheek. "Too much?"

I shrugged.

He didn't know who I really was. Sure, he'd seen my shrunken Dad and he must have known there was more to me than your average new girl in town, but he had no real idea of who I was or where I came from.

"I like you a lot," I said. He smiled. I moved a little and turned back to him, happy to have more space between us. He seemed a bit deflated but he wasn't angry.

"Liking is good."

"But you don't know me at all," I said. "I like kissing you, but I don't want to hurt you."

He smiled.

"You girls are always worried about hurting us," he said. "I'm fourteen years old. I don't care about getting hurt, unless you're planning on running me over on the old people's scooter again. That did hurt."

"I want you to know me," I said. "I want you to know my whole family, but it's been a horrible week. Not horrible, really… there's been good stuff, but I can't do this thing with you, not here on your couch."

"Not tonight, you mean?" Will said.

"Probably not."

"Gotcha popcorn," Jade said leaning over the back of the couch and plonking down two huge paper cups of popcorn. She stepped over the back of the couch and sat cross-legged next to me, cradling her own box. "So has it started yet?"

Will pulled a face at me.

"I think it'll start soon," I said. "But let's not rush things."

I reached across and took Will's hand in mine, giving it a squeeze. He pulled another face, poked out his tongue and then squeezed my hand back.

"You are a piece of work, Charlie Conti," he said.

"Thanks for moving here though," Jade said. "Henty Bay needed a little rocket like you to shake things up."

I threw some popcorn into my mouth and crunched down on the salty freshness. It felt good. Luca came bounding into the room and jumped on to the couch between Will and me, his hands diving into both our cups of popcorn.

Will upended it over Luca's head and the popcorn cascaded down his pyjama top and into my lap. I screamed (forgive me) and then Luca was climbing over me to escape Will stuffing more popcorn down his top. Jade pulled her own cup away.

"Na-uh, this stuff is too good to throw around," she said.

I clapped my hands over my eyes as Will climbed over me, chasing Luca. I screamed again but it collapsed into laughter as legs and arms entwined and the three of us rolled onto the floor, leaving Jade alone with her popcorn and a smug look on her face.

Luca scuttled away and I found myself on top of Will looking down at his face, my hair brushing against his skin. He smiled, pearly whites and those sparkling eyes. And I thought again that he was too good, too perfect.

It couldn't last. But it was what it was for now, and I was happy with that.

So no one really understands what happened that afternoon in Henty Bay, but somehow a gang of kids stopped a giant water woman from stealing a bunch of babies.

And somehow a girl called Charlie Conti managed to make some real friends and started to feel like a normal fourteen year old girl.

:BFF!! ☺

EPILOGUE

IT'S AFTER MIDNIGHT. There are some sounds out there in the darkness but otherwise I'm alone up here on the roof again. There's a light in the police station, so Mr Chase is probably still hard at work. And there's a ship sitting out in the harbour with its white lights like Christmas decorations.

I've been thinking about you for a while now, I guess. On and off all week, really, and I don't know what to do about it.

I know you're gone.

It was your choice.

You didn't ask Luca or me, or ask Dad, or even ask

yourself really. You just did it. Acted on instinct. Impulsive.

Now we have to live with the consequences.

Life doesn't have to be about sacrifices though. I've been hard on myself for ages, trying to make up for you not being here. And I've blamed myself just like Dr Chrissy said I would when I had to go see her every week last year. She's pretty cool and I miss her, but she was right that I would act out this way.

She said I'd try to become the mother.

But I don't want to be that. It's not going to help anyone. Dad doesn't need a minder - he needs to get his own life in order. And Luca doesn't need a new mum either. I can be me. I can be me, here in normal old Henty Bay. I can close my eyes and hear the waves again. And I can smell the night.

It's my moment.

And you can't take that away from me.

Of course, I underestimated you.

The shadow fell across me like a wave and I jumped back, scrambling to the window. My heart was pounding but before I reached the window I heard the familiar gruff voice of my brother - my older brother.

"Nice place," he said.

Jack was two years older than me and I hadn't seen him in years. He's tall, maybe even catching Dad and he wore a glow in the dark PacMan ghost t-shirt.

"Jack?"

"In the flesh," he said, still standing at full height, his hands in the back pockets of his jeans.

"What are you doing here?"

"I saw you on the telly," he said. "You've got older. Not wearing the pigtails anymore?"

I shook my head.

"Where's Dad?" he asked.

I didn't fully trust Jack and the way his eyes were looking beyond me, into the apartment, made me cautious. I held my breath and counted slowly to three, looking out over the rooftops.

"Around."

"I didn't see him on the news," Jack said. "Saw the Mayan Goddess thing, but it's all a bit sketchy."

"Aztec," I corrected him.

Every picture taken was hazy, probably because of Dan's powers. He sucked up a lot of electricity and that included batteries. Most phone cameras were useless and the local journalist's camera got water logged.

"Right, Aztec," Jack said. "I could tell it was you though. You've got some nifty moves and balls of steel."

"Are you staying?"

He shrugged.

"We're family," he said and took out his phone.

"Why are you really here?"

He checked messages, sighed and slipped it back into his back pocket.

"I told you," he said slowly. He seemed sad suddenly, or

tired. "Everyone knows where you are now. Everyone. And you know that's not good news for Dad. It's not good for you either, or anyone else who lives in this town."

I tried to keep calm but my face must have given it away. Jack reached out his hand and clapped me on the shoulder which was probably as close to a hug as I'd ever get from him.

"I'm just warning you, that's all."

I took a breath, trying to control the blood rushing through my body, trying to channel the quiet that was suddenly gone in my mind.

"You mean Mum don't you?" I said softly.

He nodded.

"She's not very happy, Charlie."

New Friends! 😊

Well, that's it, reader. I get a happy ending and then a cliff-hanger, but isn't that like all our lives? One thing runs into another. I can tell you that my life was never going to be about sitting by the beach and listening to Triple J's Hottest 100. I hope you enjoyed the book, and I hope you come back for the next one. It's called *Friend Zone*.

In the meantime, I'd love you to tell me how you liked it. Writing reviews keep these kinds of books out there, so please help out if you can.

And if you're interested in reading more about that Dan Galkin kid, he's got a book of his own called *The Miranda Contract*. You can read the first chapter here, but it takes place a few years after this one and Dan's grown up a bit.

Thanks again for reading about the Adventures of Charlie Conti.

See you next time!
Charlie

ABOUT THE AUTHORS

Ben Langdon was born in Geelong, Victoria, and is a graduate of Deakin University. He is the author of The Miranda Contract and The Halo Effect, editor of This Mutant Life, and a high school teacher in Portland, Victoria (which may, or may not, be the alter ego for Henty Bay).

benlangdon.net
benlangdon@kalamitypress.com
Twitter @LangdonBen

Eliza Langdon was also born in Geelong and is the daughter of Ben. After complaining that she didn't like reading books, the father and daughter team decided to write their own, featuring a spunky girl called Charlie Conti. Eliza attends Portland Secondary College and loves reading comics, cooking up storms in the kitchen, and binge-watching TV series on DVD.

elizalangdon@kalamitypress.com

ABOUT THE ILLUSTRATOR

Lorin Olsen was born and raised in New England in the United States. From the moment he was asked to draw the first picture of Charlie Conti and was given her description, he knew this was something he wanted to be part of. Lorin has a passion for drawing characters and bringing them to life, and the only thing that really comes close to his feelings about drawing is his love for teaching others what he knows. Feel free to send him an email with any questions you might have, he is always happy to help however he can.

olsenlorin@gmail.com

PREVIEW OF
THE MIRANDA CONTRACT

AVAILABLE AT KALAMITY PRESS

Chapter 1 - Dan
Present day

EVERY TIME THE doors slid back, Dan Galkin looked up expecting to see his mother, but all he got was a wintery blast of June air and the half-surprised look of customers stumbling into the shop. He waited for their orders, smiled in the right places, and took the money. The guys in the back were having all the fun, as usual; listening to music while they slipped burgers into microwaves, cracking jokes and exchanging tales at the deep fryer. And Dan was stuck at the front of shop, exposed to the public and their appetites – the 'smile until you die' job - and because he was late to work, again, he didn't know whether the others had rigged the roster or whether the world just hated him.

And then there was the thing with his mother. She'd called him that morning, all half-construed, panicked sentences and pauses that moved uncomfortably into one-sided small talk. She hadn't spoken to him in three years and Dan hated having to forget all of that to fill the gaps in their phone conversation. He hated her, or he wanted to. Then she said she would come and see him, and he didn't know whether it was just the easiest thing to say at the time, or whether she did plan to track him down to Birdie's and play the role of attentive mother over a plate of spicy chicken and a coke.

She hadn't wished him a happy birthday, probably hadn't remembered. Seventeen years old wasn't really an important one, he figured. Nothing to phone home about. Apparently.

There was a tapping at the front doors, followed by a gentle shuddering as the new kid tried to jimmy them open. He'd locked himself out of the shop – again - flipping the automatic sensors off as he sprayed and cleaned the glass panels on the outside. He'd managed to get himself locked out three times in the past fortnight which wasn't exactly a glowing recommendation. Sure, the criteria for working at Birdie's Chicken and Pizza wasn't too extensive, but the new kid seemed terminally inept. At least the locked doors kept the cold air out of the shop. Dan wanted to tell the kid to just walk away, to hang up the little cap, slide back the name badge and go home. It wasn't too late for him. He was only fifteen or something, went to the local school, had a future in some other non-fast food industry. But the kid gave him an apologetic shrug from behind the glass and Dan shook his head, secretly channelling the faintest of surges through the air and into the electronic doors which leapt back into life, parting and allowing the kid inside.

Dan wasn't like any other fast food service employee. He was uberhuman, born with a twist to his genetic code giving him the potential to develop strange and seemingly impossible gifts. In his case, Dan discovered in his eleventh year that he could change the channels on his television without using the remote. This ability grew over time so that he could eventually 'hear' the electrical world around him and in most cases he could exert some control over it.

But it wasn't like anyone knew that Dan could tell the appliances what to do, or command the doors to open and close at will. He was definitely in the 'don't ask, don't tell' camp when it came to disclosing his uberhuman abilities. In the past he had been a bit more forthcoming, but it never ended well. People were all very understanding and accepting at first, but eventually the charade crumbled and people realised he was just a freak, albeit a useful freak. Demands were made; little things like coaxing the pokie machines or just topping up bank accounts until the next pay day. Friends dropped away when the favours ended.

There were lots of other ubers though, spread across the world doing all sorts of useful things. Websites tracked their deeds, bloggers and social commentators ranked and re-ranked them, and all the while, life sort of went to crap for Dan. He was working at a place that couldn't seem to decide whether it was a pizza shop or a fried and spicy chicken place. He dropped out of school a year before, somewhere between Year 11 and 12, and was semi-squatting in an apartment with people he didn't even really know.

"Thanks, man," the new kid said, panting slightly as he stashed the cleaning stuff in the cupboard and tied on a new apron. "Won't happen again."

Dan nodded. Not convinced.

Out in the back someone laughed at a joke and he could hear the delivery drivers arriving for the Tuesday afternoon debriefing with the day manager. It was depressing, but Dan wondered whether one day he might make it as a manager. At least there was the possibility of incentive payments in management rather than minimum tips doing deliveries or the base level wage he scored at the counter.

Customers floated in, but Dan ignored them to let the new kid practise his 'smile while slowly dying inside' skills. He made himself look busy by fiddling with the drink machine, hoping the hours would suddenly melt away like the slushed ice pouring out over his hands. Instead, his phone chirped twice, vibrating in his pocket, and calling him away from sorting through the syrup dispenser. He wiped his hands dry on his apron and pulled the phone out, but it wasn't ringing. He flipped it closed again and felt the vibrations still coming from his pocket.

It was his other phone, the small black one. It wasn't the 'happy phone', that was for sure. He looked at the screen and read the caller ID: Owens. The message was simple: Office midnight.

Dan wondered whether he should just delete it.

"Dan?" the new kid nudged him and he quickly slipped the phone back into his pocket, wiping his hands again on his apron. "You've got a … a customer," the new kid said, looking confused.

The woman wasn't a customer. She wore a stretchy black and red striped long sleeve top which almost covered her hands, and a straw hat and shades which almost covered her face. After nodding in a vague way, she turned and found a seat at one of the booths commonly used by school girls to discuss the day's events and bitch about their friends and family. Dan wondered whether he could sneak out the back and disappear into the streets, but the new kid blocked his way, the confused smile still playing on his face.

"Man, she's got like…" he said softly, looking down at his hands with wide eyes. "You think she's here for the Human Tour?"

"What?" Dan pulled his eyes away from the woman.

"Miranda Brody's concert, you know? The Human Tour."

He moved past the kid and walked towards the booth, noticing how she hadn't really changed much in the years he'd been in the city. Her hair was a little drier than usual, and her arms were bony, but he couldn't remember a time when she wasn't thin and brittle. Handle with care, they always used to say.

Dan sat down but kept his hands in his lap.

"I didn't think you were really coming," he said.

She smiled, awkwardly, and looked down at her hands, rubbing each finger, easing the aches. The flecked blue skin was dry, like her wiry hair and chipped nails. When she noticed Dan watching her, she pulled her sleeves longer and cupped the hands away out of sight. Her body seemed to shrink away from the harsh lights, the straw hat giving her some refuge from stares and open-mouthed looks. Over at the counter, the new kid took orders in between glances at the freakish blue-skinned woman.

"I'm your mother," she said in a raspy voice. "Of course I would come."

"Seriously?" Dan said.

She pulled her hands out of sight into her own lap, her shoulders dropping. She turned her head and looked out of the window, which gave Dan a glimpse of her profile. Hawkish nose, old tortoise-shell shades, cracked lips.

"It's been…" she stalled.

"Three years," Dan finished for her.

"Difficult," she said, not looking back. "When your … father died, I … well, I didn't cope very well, Danny."

She hadn't coped very well her entire life. At sixteen her skin blistered and peeled, revealing a bluish hue underneath that never washed away no matter how hard she scrubbed, no matter how many lotions she applied. Dan's father, the less than impressive Nico, knocked her up in the first few weeks of courting and then managed to get himself arrested for a half-arsed bank robbery. So, no, Theresa Galkin hadn't coped very well at all with life.

"I guess not," Dan said.

"You are doing well," she said softly. He couldn't tell whether it was a question or an opinion. He pulled off his Birdie's cap and tossed it on the table. His mother's head turned back from the window and looked at the cap.

"I'm not dead, I guess," he said.

She swallowed, her neck bird-like as she tried to compose herself.

"It's been difficult," she said again, rehearsing her lines.

A group of school kids took up a second booth near Dan and he heard them chattering about their lives, about music and boys and girls and homework and holidays.

"Your grandfather is back," she said.

Dan watched her lips. They were pressed tightly together, not quite hiding the hate she must have been tasting.

His grandfather had returned. From the dead.

It wasn't that he couldn't believe what she said. People like his grandfather never really took death seriously. Dan just didn't know how he felt about the development. Five years before, his grandfather had been everything to him. He had been the stand-in father when the real one was locked in prison. He had been the only calm influence the night Dan's body started sucking up all the electricity in the house. He had become the confidant, the teacher. And eventually the betrayer.

"Great," Dan said, grabbing his cap and standing up. "Maybe we could have a happy family dinner one night?"

He walked back to the counter, blinking hard against the flashes of light in his eyes. Sometimes when he was stressed the electrical charges his body generated would try to burst out of him, to unleash themselves on the world and cause havoc and destruction. Sometimes his body wanted to become the weapon his grandfather trained him for. But Dan didn't have to do what anyone said anymore. He wasn't a pawn in the old man's game; it had already been played out. And Dan lost.

"Next?" he asked, a little too fiercely, as he checked into the console next to the new kid.

A couple slipped into line and started to discuss the menu. Dan felt the console humming beneath his fingers.

He followed the couple's discussion, bringing up their orders, revising them, adding all sorts of extras as they casually changed their minds. His fingers didn't move but the orders entered directly from minuscule surges from his mind.

"Take your time," Dan said, forcing a smile. They didn't even hear him.

And suddenly Dan's mother was at the counter, her bony blue fingers clutching the edge of the formica bench top. She wasn't tall, but she leaned across so that she was directly in Dan's space. Her eyes were bare now, the shades discarded. The whites were yellowish, bloodshot.

"You have a choice," she hissed. Her breath was stale. How long had she been locked up inside, he wondered; his thoughts leaving the console and harking back to when he lived with her in the beach house. "You don't have to live like me."

She turned on the young couple, whipping her hat off and tossing it away to her right. She leered at them, her frizzy dead hair and her flaky blue face too much to ignore. In a second she swept her head towards the school kids and snarled at them, her dark blue lips pulled back to reveal the jagged yellow teeth. She played the wicked witch, the crazy blue skinned woman, the insane uberhuman freak.

Dan stepped back, away from the whirling confrontation. The people in lines scuttled to each side and his mother swayed a little more before retreating to the sliding doors. She looked back at him, teeth still bared, but there was sadness there in her eyes. She pointed a finger at him.

"You have been chosen," she said. "You can be more… so much more."

And then she was gone, pushing through the automatic doors when they didn't open quickly enough, and out into the street.

"Man," the new kid said. "That is weird shit."

Dan just shrugged.

Customers shook themselves back into line and some of the workers from out the back came into the front wondering what the crazy customer had done. The manager was on a cigarette break, but later she would curse herself for missing the action. Not much exciting ever happened at Birdie's.

'The Miranda Contract' is available now!